Blood Virgin

The Hazing (Volume I)

J K Aston

ISBN: 0692824286
ISBN 13: 9780692824283

Dedication

To all who seek refreshment from the purifying fountain of love's youthfulness.

He accepted all the parts of her that she denied, and from that she learned to love them too.

A.J. Lawless

1

A freak summer hail storm pelted the residents of Saint Germaine.

Birds dropped like flies in midair when hit by volleys of ice. At least humans were able to scramble for shelter.

But Gretchen couldn't hide.

The vehicle slid on a sheet of black ice, settling into a cockamamie position—between the shoulder and fast lane.

The engine died.

She stumbled out, shaking her fists heavenward. *Is that the best you can do, God? I've got to be places!*

A young girl popped out from behind a construction pylon. "Ms. Lanners, um, can I call you Gretchen? Sorry to scare you."

"Little miss, you amuse me. What ya doin' here? And how'd you know my name?"

"Simple, it's all written in the scrolls."

Gretchen cast a dazed look.

The girl reached into her blouse pocket and offered a rag to sponge off the moisture.

"No thanks, little thing. *You're* the one wet behind the ears."

"Ma'am, I didn't realize you're so cynical."

"Never mind, child. Where's your mommy and daddy? Go home before I call the cops and report you as a runaway."

Traffic was at a standstill behind them.

"My name's Naomi. I'm actually one hundred twenty years old. The tempest? Well, it's all I could do to get your attention."

"Huh? Such big words kiddo, but I'm still not impressed."

Gretchen charged back to her truck all jittery. She straddled the door frame spread eagle. Splotches of makeup leaked down her face.

"Ma'am, I read your mind earlier. Jake Conroe wants to see you."

Gretchen hesitated, slid her jaw and dragged an angry glare at Naomi.

"What? How'd you know Jake? Oh, a practical joker? I'm getting slaughtered in this icy mess and you're disrespecting the dead. How dare you!"

The weather was taking its toll.

She flicked back her stringy hair to size up the kid. "Hell, you're not worth my time, child."

Gretchen slammed the door, thumped on the gas and rode that truck like a bucking bronco.

Jake. Jake. Jake.

Damn captivating. Gnawing on my brain like a termite.

During their fleeting life together, Jake Conroe satisfied her more than all the other beaus. Gretchen had claimed him as her exclusive, hunky trophy. Those moonlit nights were fantastic. He'd proposed three times, but she always had some shitty excuse. He was bigger than life to her, even now as she dealt with the loss all over again.

Pull yourself together and drive, bitch!

To shirk the pain, Gretchen fled past abandoned cotton gin towns, crisscrossing turnpikes and desolate ranchlands. Hours became minutes.

Destination nowhere.

Groggily she drifted into the path of an oncoming big rig. The driver pounded the horn. Gretchen jerked the steering wheel, barely avoiding a collision.

I've gotta clear my mind before I kill myself.

She pulled over at the entrance to a memorial park. The dashboard clock: 11:36 PM. She cut off the engine.

Man, I need a smoke, but my wobbly hands won't cooperate.

A mysterious heirloom laying on the passenger seat distracted her.

Hmm, scrumptious lily white fabric...Yummy scent, like a root beer float.

The words, 'Celebrate newness of life. MENDERS will guide to your dead lover's heartbeat,' were smeared in blood.

Where the fuck did this come from? You're losing it girl! No cell coverage and no fuel!

She yanked up the odd braid of cloth — *Hell, it's a scarf. I'll use it to flag someone on the highway.*

An unknown source of something.

A twitching, erogenous sensation spread across Gretchen's middle-aged body. Her breasts went supple and her nipples erect, suck-able and playful.

Now tight abs, ripples of muscles replaced the flab. A warm throbbing desire, searching for satisfaction. Purified, glowing skin.

One quick look at myself...I'll be damned!

In the rearview mirror—the reflection—a girl identical to me; age twenty, half a lifetime ago. Snowy complexion, cascading brunette hair, no wrinkles. A virgin Rapunzel princess, a re-creation of my girlish innocence? Ha-ha, my mind's on fire!

Totally wildfire.

Whoa. Like I asked for this? I could be a cover model! No goddamn way! Whatever the spell, it's flirting with my youthfulness. I'm as yummy as a bowl of peaches and cream though.

But still an old soul.

I'm sitting here dog-tired, talking to myself? These changes to my body—some crazy ass curse! Payback for a previous sin? Why am I so new, so sexy and gorgeous? That little be-witcher cunt Naomi changed me! But hey, at least I look young again!

2

Gretchen was reared in a poverty-stricken suburb of Houston, the youngest of four sisters.

Her parents were always absent, working menial jobs to support them. Dad and mom appointed Callie, the eldest, to raise her.

Gretchen was a *paper bag princess*, never satisfied, always yearning, ashamed of her upbringing, lusting after the fineries of life.

Her thirsty soul brought her to this place.

"How do you like your new phantom body, Gretchen?" a calming voice from outside the vehicle announced.

She fumbled at the flashlight, but the fresh batteries were drained.

From the shadows a man almost half her age appeared, sporting a headband. He cut a rugged, handsome figure.

Gretchen swallowed. Dry saliva cracked at her throat.

His essence, a mere illusion? I wanna know more...

"I'm real, I'm your Jake," he proclaimed.

Gretchen processed his words, noticed his headband was just a knotty scarf —akin to hers. Bailing out of the truck and sprinting over, pointing her finger like a school teacher.

"That Naomi's some illusionist! She must've distracted me, snuck around and dumped it inside."

Jake nodded smugly.

She paused.

"Is this your way of saying a final howdy and goodbye, Jake? Shoal Creek didn't kill you after all?"

"Yeah, but not in the way you think."

Jake puffed up his peacock attitude and paraded over.

Closer...

"Gretchen baby, touch me," he pleaded.

She knew how to hook a man, but unlike the skanks and cougars in her hometown, she never gave in on the first date.

Her indifference worked. Jake planted a sweet kiss squarely on her left cheek.

The heart aching from three unfilled years without him made her lose control. A tumult of emotions fueled the fire of attraction within their guts.

They embraced, foreheads pressed together. Gretchen's teardrops were a pageantry of unearthly delights; brilliantly shaped rhinestones, cascading to the ground and forming puddles.

He tenderly held Gretchen's hands and kissed the tops of them.

Memories gushed out, uncontrollable, heartfelt.

They met years earlier while standing in line at the Saint Germaine drug store. Gretchen was refilling her Oxycodone prescription. He knew then she was a vulnerable princess.

Eye-to-eye again in this deserted countryside. Both reformed and vulnerable to the touch.

"Do you like the changes, Gretchen?"

She broke into a hysterical chuckle.

"Whoa, yeah! You're a damn ruse!"

"Sweetheart, this is no dream. Granted we're sure young again. Let's make the best of tonight, okay?"

"That child Naomi spouted over being older than she looked, and now you assert you've risen from the grave. This Peter Pan and Tinkerbell shit has to stop."

Jake presented Gretchen a three-year-old pic from the funeral parlor. It was a selfie she snapped while hunched over kissing his embalmed body, a romantic memento placed in the casket before he was sealed.

"Oh my God! Where'd you get this?"

"My love, don't you recall our precious keepsakes? I asked you a third time to marry me, but then, um, Shoal Creek."

"Grave robber! You unearthed the pic!"

Gretchen's grief boiled over. Her mind replayed the sad times from years earlier. Jake had been killed, disfigured beyond recognition by the petroleum tanker's explosion at Shoal Creek overpass.

Who is this man?

Undaunted, he convinced her to follow along a footpath which meandered through high brush and into a meadow. Ahead one-hundred paces stood the old Burkburnett graveyard; at row thirty-nine, plot seven, was his entombment.

Or so Gretchen thought.

The night became alive. Slight breezes teased the wild grasses to roll in waves. The midsummer night moonbeams breached a Bois d'Arc tree's drowsy branches, casting the illusion of yellow eye sockets staring out from within miniature skulls figures.

Eeriness pervaded the crypts.

"Stand back, Gretchen!"

She was baffled.

A small animal scurried in front of them.

"Watch those wispy apparitions circle us! Don't worry, though," he reassured. "It's just another *Gatherer*."

"What are Gatherers?" She asked timidly.

The Gatherers hover, searching for *grief sickness*. They snatch up living people's hair and return to the Menders habitat to harvest the particles. That's all Naomi would tell me."

Gretchen was expressionless.

Jake's inner self *probed things.* Reality became clear to him, only he could identify the Gatherers. Gretchen hadn't crossed through the Hazing portal yet and was lacking spirit ripeness.

"Babe, I apologize for confusing you, but Naomi's prophecy is weak concerning you."

Jake hastily swung open the creaky gargoyle gates of the old Burkburnett Cemetery. The commotion flushed out the pigeons nesting in the maintenance barn.

In the course of three short years, the graveyard had lost its southern charm. An untidy sight, headstones weathered and cracked, prickly weeds flourished. A creature had been munching feverishly on animal bones and littering the area to mark its territory.

"Gretchen, an imposing element's overtaken this place. Watch the shifty moonlight, the ground's alive with hope. Souls who're separated from their lovers by tragic death are eligible for the Hazing. Naomi's a Mender high priestess who unites with the Gatherers to become otherworldly matchmakers."

"Conjuring things just to scare me, Jake?"

"No, only stating truth. Do you still love me, babe?"

"Stop the morbid crap and I might. If you have special powers, then fill my gas tank and drive me home."

"It's impossible, at least for now."

"Why not?"

"I'm unable to leave this place and be with you until we're *fulfilled.* I can't make love to you the same way as before, but only in a *fourth dimension* sort of way, where love can't be separated by time or space."

"Huh? Spooky talk, Jake, get real."

"I'm as real as it gets, babe. Just try to understand me. My world is thriving with pleasure. I can transport you to the next level."

He baffled her.

"Sweetheart, your hesitation's a natural response. Will you gamble on me?"

She acknowledged apprehensively.

He tied the scarf over her eyes.

Blind faith.

"Gretchen, I'm gonna lay some good juju on you. The timing's perfect to make amends. Listen and learn from the noises here."

"Huh?"

"Babe, every time you hear bellowing frogs in the mating pond, a coyote's howling before its fangs bite into rabbit flesh, or an owl's pitiful hoot to advertise its lethal strike upon the field mice, be assured the Gatherers are hot on the trail for new recipients."

He firmly took Gretchen's hand and recited, "Powerful Menders, captivate Gretchen Lanners with pleasurable and sumptuous scenes. Carry my beloved back in time, where glowing eyes and heart bind with tears. Wandering amongst the spicy, irrevocable memories of the past tragedies to find comfort. A treasure will appear. Invoke the innermost desires on her lover, for he'll be waiting."

3

*C*ampsite at Bois d'Arc Lake, late summer, three years earlier.

"Babe, look at the skies. There's a falling comet! It must have our names written on it!"

"God, you're so romantic, Jake. Maybe we should sleep out here under the stars instead of in the tent."

"Such a tempting thought. Stoke the fire with more embers and cuddle me, sweetie. Those fireflies are dancing and celebrating life. They only generate the light for a few days, stoking their bellies with nectar from the earth. Life is short but happy for them."

"We're mere tenderfoots in these woods, Jake. Let's play hooky so you don't have to go outta town on business tomorrow? You belong here next to me, stud muffin."

"I'll only be gone for two weeks. You know the drill, baby. Our time apart gets you so wet...keep that landing strip nicely maintained and I'll promise my perpetually hard dick will be yours again."

Gretchen blushed and smacked Jake's ass while he was preparing the S'mores over the slowly diminishing cinders.

The razzing continued late into the night.

Jake pulled out a flask from his backpack. It was a damn good concoction. Shots of the spiced rum masked the pain of the couple's impending farewell. They reveled in it while reclining in their camp chairs, sipping and cheering to the bounties of life.

It was nearly dawn. Jake was out like a light, but Gretchen fended off her drowsiness.

The corner of her eye caught the unmistakable image of a timeworn lady scampering around a nearby campsite. Her worldly belongings were heaped into a rickety shopping cart.

The public park was a magnate for the homeless, crackheads and lowlifes. It was common for vagrants to invade the trash bins and fish off the boat landing, but the old lady was different.

Gretchen nudged Jake. "Wake up! Look there, she's using some big-ass spoons to stir a recipe."

They stood up and pretended to mess with the ice chest and get a better angle.

Then...swoop!

Something with talons, arced wings and gleaming eyes hurled from the dark sky.

"Stop it! Oh my God! Jake, help me!"

The feathery attacker scuffled with Gretchen's hair.

Jake swung a camp shovel, but the *bird object* was too nimble.

Gretchen's scalp felt like burning coals. Splotches of blood seeped down her forehead.

Jake grabbed a first aid kit and tended to her wound. The lantern's light revealed a few superficial abrasions, but nothing major.

"Sweetie, you'll be fine. What on earth possessed that unrelenting bird to pounce on your lovely head?"

"Your guess is as good as mine. It was an airborne entity. I could feel it lock on and rip me apart."

She felt around. "Shit, I'm missing gobs of curls."

"Maybe it mistook your locks for tree branches or twigs. Probably a momma bird trying to build her nest," he suggested.

With daybreak nearing, Jake readied the campsite and started packing.

"We should warn the old lady about the air assaults, she could be the next target," Gretchen proposed.

"Knock yourself out," he said.

"Pardon me over there, whatever your name is!" Gretchen yelled fervently. "Be on the lookout for aggressive owls!"

The hag was immovable, void of expression. Within seconds, a beautiful white turtle dove landed gracefully on her shoulder. She petted it and took an article from its beak.

"Are you deaf?" Gretchen blurted.

The woman pasted a haughty look and muttered some chants.

Gretchen grabbed the lantern and strode over to introduce herself. When the light was sufficiently bright, Gretchen exploded in disgust. She recognized the face, but not the withered body.

"Naomi? Is that you? What a fuckin' coincidence! You indwelling bitch! Jake, Naomi's living in an old woman's body!"

Within seconds, waves of fog blanketed everything. Bois d'Arc Lake, the old woman, even her beloved Jake vanished like a magic act. Only silence and darkness remained.

4

Gretchen woke up. Romeo the pet Rottweiler was licking her face. He'd been grinding on a grisly looking chew toy. It was a half-decomposed animal femur.

"Gretchen, you've been sweating like a pig, twitching violently in your sleep for the past twelve hours."

Callie offered her a glass of water.

Gretchen looked offended.

"Where's my cell phone?"

"Chill sis, it was buzzing unmercifully all night. I'd turn it off, but minutes later it would recover on its own, then generate a strange humming sound. It must have a bad battery. I stuffed it under a pillow to drown it so I could sleep."

Callie's nose picked up a scent in the air.

Gretchen caught a whiff of it as well.

"Yeah, Callie, I need a bath.

"You smell like a dude, Gretchen."

She scurried to the restroom.

I thought I got rid of all his personal effects after the funeral.

She checked under the sink for more evidence, and found Jake's body spray had recently been tampered with.

Ghosts in my attic?

"He *did* visit me! I'm not jacked up after all!"

Déjà vu.

"Callie, you may have *thought* it was me laying here, but a part of me ran away to be with Jake last night. I took the truck and..."

"You went to his grave site?"

"Much more than that. We've been talking about hooking up again."

"Um, Jake's been dead for years, Gretchen."

"Not anymore! I'll prove it."

She cast a wistful glance at the vanity mirror.

Damnit! My face and body look middle-aged again. Ugh.

"Sorry to burst your bubble Gretchen, but you're thirty-three, remember?"

Her hair was full of rats' nests.

Callie took hold of a brush and stroked Gretchen's hair to calm her angst. She combed up loose clumps, uncovering a bald spot near the crown of Gretchen's head.

"Sis, you're losing your hair due to all the tension."

Goose bumps.

"Callie, it's just like my dream at that lake! The goddamn owl was real!"

"Don't panic!" Callie assured. "You never left this house last night. I flipped on the security system."

Romeo growled at something behind them.

The fur on his back stood straight up. Gretchen called him over to scratch his ears.

"I'm fully aware you miss Jake, but allowing memorabilia to resurface isn't helping you heal."

"Huh?"

"Pardon me for being nosey, but your den bookshelf has an 8-by-10 framed picture of you two. I noticed it for the first time last night when I walked past the room."

Callie's face didn't lie.

Gretchen stormed into the den. Callie followed like a lost puppy.

Gretchen studied the portrait.

'Celebrate newness of life. MENDERS will guide to your dead lover's heartbeat,' was etched on the frame.

Disbelief filled her eyes.

"I only snapped one pic and put it in Jake's coffin. Where did this phony image come from? It's horrid of Jake. He's smirking at the camera. Red lipstick's smudged all over his dead face! People will get the wrong impression."

Gretchen searched her mind.

Funny, Naomi's scarf has the identical saying written on it. And I never wear red lipstick, only purple lip gloss. Naomi's fucking with my mind again, but for the record, her curses on me are better than Botox injections.

Big sister warned Gretchen to lose the picture, but she refused; Callie made some popcorn, turned on a comedy show as a deterrent from all the drama.

The hours whittled away.

A peculiar clicking sound emanated from the den. Romeo's snarling roused Gretchen's interest.

She nudged Callie, but sis wouldn't budge.

Here we go again. Another paranormal event. Hell, even my sex toys might start levitating before the night's over. I need my studly lover back so badly, I'm ready to believe anything!

She returned to the den with Romeo in tow.

The closest door was gaping open. Romeo's ears perked up, as though spotting a familiar presence. He darted inside the dark firmament. Gretchen tried to catch him, but too late. His husky canine body was engulfed.

A reddish orb arose from nowhere. It produced a source of calming energy. Several vertical and horizontal patterns crisscrossed in the center, opening up like a kaleidoscope.

A transient passageway between death and life, suffering and pleasure.

Bewildered, Gretchen melted to the floor. Waves of mist rolled in. An invisible force lifted her. She transcended into the night sky. From her vantage point, shimmering towns and country landscapes came and went at lightning speeds. The enchanted shawl protected her hair, so as not a single pretty strand would be disturbed by the chaos.

A new realm. A new body.

Time and space no longer mattered. She glided in puffy air, the perfect organism, breathing from her skin and not her mouth.

Gretchen's new consciousness urged her on. Celestial forms, palettes of tranquility and harmony, tempted her to explore the newborn happiness.

Sedated by the opiate of flawless primordial love, a trace of *him* blasted her thoughts.

I've landed in paradise!

Faithful pooch Romeo greeted her. A red bandana was tied around his neck. His blissful vibes tempted her to stroll unconfined, fleeing her past inner life of misery and grief.

The pilgrimage was a delectable jaunt into the wilderness. Her body itched for human pleasure.

An emerald pathway opened into a mountain clearing where a majestic château biosphere hovered in the silky-smooth clouds, bounded by snowcapped mountaintops, a haven where dreams intersect reality.

A massive medieval castle draw bridge invited her in.

Gretchen ambled through a sparkling vestibule where fresh spring aquifers bubbled lively.

Enthralled, she surveyed a lagoon-like structure. Sunken candelabras glimmered, illuminating the watery cavern. Delicate harmonies danced deftly, like butterflies in a patch of sunflowers. A watery plume gushed down into the center from somewhere above.

Erotic destination.

At closer glance, the physique of a perfectly crafted man, *her man*, came into view.

His virile voice commanded and agitated her blood.

"Baby, strip down to your angelic flesh and come embrace me. The Gatherers lit this place with torches to honor your return."

A strange silhouette appeared. Its form was androgynous.

"Jake, I'm finally able to see what you see! Is it a Gatherer?"

"I'm Murtha the Gatekeeper," it announced. "Welcome to the Mender habitat."

Gretchen wasted no time. She untied the scarf, disrobed and handed Murtha her garments.

She waded out to the waterfall where he was standing.

Here was the ex-lover she never planned on marrying. But now as a supernatural duo, they could be formidable.

The liquid was not water at all. It consisted of a sensual, warm oil and aromatic lotion to awaken the goddess in her.

"Jake, I succumbed to drugs and men in your absence after you died on me. I lined them up, strung them along, and expected different results, but all I got was emptiness. I've been searching for my Knight in Shining Armor, injecting needles into my body which tore holes, but that didn't solve anything. If I could discover an *elixir* which reignites my passion for life, I'll be good again. I lacked the bravery to change until you stepped into my dreams. Tell me this is no dream! Please Jake!"

Suspended in midair, two ivory turtledoves, positioned on each side of a tulip-shaped glass goblet, fluttered toward Gretchen. Their fragile beaks clasped the pair of aquamarine gold leaf dragon handles. A hand painted red musk rose wrapped around its stem.

Jake's deep toned macho voice said, "Drink this cup's blessing and be pleased."

He took the chalice and offered her a sip. The smell and taste of the liquid reminded Gretchen of a root beer float. They cheered to the present and to the future.

He draped his muscular arms around her waist, while his strong fingers massaged her back.

Their libidos discharged carnal vibes and forbidden desires.

Only a loin cloth separated his manhood from her view. She groped his tight butt cheeks, guiding his well hung hardness toward her bubble butt.

Gretchen allowed him to land love bites on her neck and strum her inner thighs while he maneuvered into position. His bulging instrument wedged between her ass cheeks. The lion's head teased her wet lips just enough...

She started sobbing and turned around to face him. "I have to go back, don't I?"

"Yes, but it's gonna be alright, baby," he assured. "Thanks to Naomi and the Menders, you're experiencing the *authentic me* for the first time in three longs years. I love you beyond words; sorry to be such a flirt, but I wanted you to get a taste of our future potential together."

"Just a *taste*? Are you refusing to bed me, Jake?"

"No, I mean the chalice. The life here is one of unending kinky, raw sex, reserved exclusively for soul mates—sucking down expensive hooch, shopping sprees in Paris, London and New York, and travel to exotic oceanside destinations on a whim. I'm hollow without you. I'm pushing hard for you to join me permanently. Can you handle it?"

"Yes baby, I have the faith to endure any struggle."

"Good! Naomi's your channel back to Saint Germaine. Once you attain spirit ripeness, and your earthen body interconnects mine in every way, we'll become a *unity*. Returning to the grave's no longer an option for me."

5

Resuming life in Saint Germaine, Gretchen was hell bent on reviving her own soul—how it ticked, and whether a potential future existed with *him*.

Saint Germaine was tucked away in the Hill Country, founded in 1865 as a mining village, known for precious gems, agates, and crystals bountifully extracted from its clefts. All that remained was a cluster of half-abandoned shacks, a souvenir from its boom days.

Miranda, a well-respected psychic, met up with Gretchen at *True Bloods*, a renovated turn of the century saloon. In contrast to Gretchen, who came from big city life, Miranda had been born and raised in Saint Germaine, and knew the locals like the back of her hand. Miranda had grabbed national recognition for solving a recent murder—exposing a criminal drug ring posing as a pagan cult to enslave runaways and prostitutes.

"Miranda, I've allowed huge doubts about my dead lover to creep up lately," Gretchen stated. "It's really getting out of control."

"Pardon my brutal honesty, girl, but you look like a rag doll. Maybe I can help shed some light on your struggles. Let's discuss your recent dreams."

"Fine. My imagination's playing tricks on me. It always happens at night."

"What does?"

"I enter a time warp and get transformed into young hot fuckable prey, then lose it all after I leave *his* presence. Bouncing around between two worlds is annoying as hell."

Miranda explored Gretchen's mind.

"Okay. Have you noticed any stigmatic manifestations, proving that you've crossed over?"

"Hell yeah, does this welt on my head qualify?"

Gretchen hunched over to display the missing hair and raw scalp.

"Look, that flying creature dived into me. It'll take weeks to grow back. I resemble a swamp cat."

"Honestly, Gretchen, nothing's out of place."

"I'm not dreaming!"

"It's alright, Gretchen. Any casual hallucinogenic drug-use?"

"Of course not! What are you implying? Christ, I've been clean for over a year. See, no new scars..."

"Other than Jake who's assumed to be dead, has anybody substantiated or been privy to your paranormal outpourings?"

"Yeah, for sure."

"Who?"

"My sister Callie combed out chunks of my loose hair."

"Think more carefully. Any other onlookers?"

"Well, my dog Romeo reappears in dreams, along with this weird ass hieroglyphic scarf."

"Can I see it?" Miranda asked cynically.

Gretchen rummaged around, reaching into her handbag.

"I've been stowing this on my person, like a pack of tampons during my period."

Miranda examined the object from head to toe.

"Gretchen, I hate to break the news, but it's nothing more than a scruffy sweatband. You may be experiencing a delusional episode. I'm unequipped to counsel you on psychosomatic disorders."

Gretchen sobbed.

Miranda plopped down some cash to pay the tab, then stood up, giving Gretchen a hug. "Sweetie, I'm sorry."

She walked away, nearing the exit.

Frantic, Gretchen screamed out, "Celebrate newness of life. MENDERS will guide to your dead lover's heartbeat!"

Miranda froze in her steps. Her face was pallor.

She humbly returned to the booth.

"Where'd you learn that phrase, Gretchen?"

"The words are a revelation. I hear Jake's voice say that my pain killers and opiates won't help with the guilt. Some girl named Naomi gave me this 'scruffy sweatband' a few days ago. That's when everything intensified at the cemetery."

"Guilt? What guilt, Gretchen?"

"I could have stopped him from leaving."

"Leaving where?"

"Miranda, promise you won't record what I'm about to tell you."

"Of course not, Gretchen. We're in this together."

"Okay.

"So tell me about Jake. Is he the source of your guilt?"

"No, I am."

Gretchen cried. Miranda handed her a tissue.

"If this is too much, sweetie, we can stop."

"No, I blame myself for Jake's condition. The camping trip at Bois d'Arc Lake three years ago—I ignored *the premonition*. I should've taken the keys away from him. He was leaving out of town the next day and was so distracted and upset at me."

"What happened at the lake?"

"A bunch of things. That camping trip was the last night I saw him alive, at least in his material body."

"Tell me more, please."

"Well, in the dream I blacked out right after I saw Naomi's face attached to that old lady's body. I was hoping to reverse the tragedy."

"What tragedy?"

"Um, where I get angry and stab Jake with a hunting knife. It was a superficial wound, but it pissed him off enough to leave me behind while he sped off into oblivion."

"He abandoned you, Gretchen?"

"In more than one way, yeah. After the wreck, his family sued the driver of the tanker, but it was my fault. I'm slowly going insane...imagining that scary Naomi...and that owl and dove hovering around...fuck, I guess it all started with the texting."

"Texting?"

"Yeah, while we were packing to leave the campsite, he carelessly laid the cell face up on the picnic table for me to see. He saved her name as *Tommie*. That hoe had the nerve to text him pictures of her boobs with a string of heart emojis. I was so heated, I threw it in the lake and lunged at him."

"I'm sorry you're under huge strain, Gretchen. In your state of being, it's virtually impossible to discern truth from fiction. Some entity's attempting to deceive you big time."

"You mean in a paranormal sort of way?" Gretchen asked.

"Yes, in ancient Druid lore, they're called *Ruffians*, depraved beings who get thrills by tricking you into thinking your true love is waiting on the other side, but the reunification never comes. You languish in despair, and are tempted to commit grievous acts."

"What kind of acts?"

"Like poisoning a lover and then staging his or her death as a suicide, one of many examples. Why'd you ask?"

"Cause since Jake died, all I've ever wanted is to rush back into his arms again. I swore to make peace when the casket was sealed, but now these twisted visits. I'm like some fly, seeing the flyswatter come at me in slow motion, then freezing up and getting smacked."

Gretchen felt Miranda's steel blue eyes scrutinize her.

"I don't blame you for giving up on me, Miranda. I'm a desperate case."

"I won't, baby girl. In fact my mood ring's picking up a signal right now...not sure where the source is coming from."

Miranda's hands patted around the inside of her small handbag. "Here, Gretchen, this is my last option."

She pulled out a necklace and flung a foreboding smirk at Gretchen.

"Do you like it?"

Gretchen was stunned.

"Oh my God, it's gorgeous! It's a keeper!"

"Right? An old lady was peddling precious rocks downtown. This rare specimen cried out my name. It's a classy stone."

"What type of rock is it?"

A Lepidolite crystal. It contains metaphysical properties, has a calming effect and wards off addictions."

Miranda delicately strung it around Gretchen's neck.

The stone necklace unlocked secrets. Gretchen witnessed naked truth.

Before their eyes, the scarf morphed into a *circlet*, a royal crown which a medieval princess or queen would wear; flushed in gold and jewel rivets, exceedingly pure and exquisite.

Gretchen celebrated.

"My vision's finally unblocked! Miraculous!"

"Gretchen, there's a significance to these happenings —every time you're transported into that dreamy place to meetup with Jake, you're changed into a sexy young goddess to fulfill some special higher destiny."

"Yeah, I radiate an irresistibility and charisma, similar to an infatuation."

"Good depiction, but my guess is you're functioning as some sort of pheromone homing beacon. To put it bluntly, you're a metaphysical seductress, but your narcissistic episodes are suppressing you from achieving true satisfaction."

"What the fuck? Stop the scientific bullshit and speak plainly, Miranda!"

"Putting it another way, why did the Egyptians embalm King Tut and pay homage after his death? They stocked his tomb with poetic verses and rare treasures. His body was vulnerable and needed to be protected until the afterlife, where he could enter the Fields of Aaru, the Egyptian heaven, to celebrate newness of life. The blood creed written on your headband is a similar prayer. You're royalty, sweetheart. Make the best of it."

"Yeah, buddy...so you're gonna start bowing down and referring to me by my new name, Princess Nefertiti?"

"Ha ha. Seriously Gretchen, you have greater metaphysical powers than me, yet you refuse to practice the art. You could've saved Jake, but were too damn skeptical, afraid of your own reflection. You're an *ecothermic* woman, possessing the ability to regulate your obsessive nature by *exchanging* love energies with Jake. You grow stronger together, a sure indication of *soul mate* love."

"Cool, but I wish Jake would stop fronting me during our height of foreplay, he's pissing me the fuck off. He holds more powers than me."

"The dichotomy of your two worlds are on a collision course, Gretchen. Sounds like Naomi started the shit storm, so firstly we need to sort out issues between you two. She's operating as either a shadow entity or schizophrenic aberration. Time to reenter *Ground Zero* and figure it all out."

6

A few nights later, Miranda and Gretchen dashed to Burkburnett graveyard like hound dogs on the hunt.

The crescent moon slumbered in the dusky sky, dispersing its lunar glow earthward.

They noticed an old man kneeling at one of the grave sites, performing a candle light vigil.

His wailing caught their ears.

"I commit my frail body to you, my precious Alice. We'll be together soon. So many years since you've passed. You bore me three beautiful children and were my soul mate in life. Gosh, you'd be so proud of our five wonderful grandchildren, they're almost all grown up! And I've kept the lake house immaculate waiting for your return. Every night I sit out on the boat dock, carving you a rosewood heart pendant. With each stroke of my knife, I dream of our happiest moments, forty-eight years now. Oh Alice, I yearn for springtime and the new life it brings. You and I spent our honeymoon on the lake, remember? I've made up the bed all comfy, picked two polyantha red roses from the garden—the kind you like best—and put on some soothing jazz in our bungalow. Soon we'll spend eternity together relishing in each other's love, frolicking under that big goose comforter."

His heart fell silent. The pause was painfully long.

Without hesitation he displayed a razor blade, ritualistically slicing open his right hand. He rubbed them together, pressing the splotchy blood onto his dead lover's headstone.

Gretchen jumped out of her skin and nearly screamed, but Miranda restrained her.

He reaffirmed hopefulness, "Alice Townsend, celebrate newness of life. MENDERS will guide to your dead lover's heartbeat."

Miranda cleared her throat, but Gretchen beat her to the punch.

"Hey Mister! Sorry to interrupt, but who taught you the saying? Please understand, we're not trying to be nosey or disrespectful of your loss..."

Gretchen's outburst throttled him.

"Well uh, good evening, young ladies, with whom do I have the pleasure of speaking?"

"Oh, so sorry, sir. My name's Gretchen Lanners, and um, my friend here is Miranda."

The man extended his right arm toward Gretchen.

She refused to shake hands.

"Don't you need a bandage on that wound, old man? It's kind of messy."

He showed them his open hand. There were no blade or blood imprints. Nothing but his veiny, leathery skin stood out.

"May I inspect?" Miranda asked.

"Yes, have at it."

She fondled his hand looking for signs.

"Do you come here often, Mister?"

"Call me Harrold, um, Harrold Townsend. I'm part of this place now. No fretting on my account."

"Okay Harrold. I'm a psychic from Saint Germaine. I hate to pry, but how'd you manage to hide your injuries?"

"Young woman, I'm not being branded by some malicious intent, and my body's still capable of registering pain."

"So you're a self-healer?"

"I'm sure it's all an illusion. Look ladies, I'm simply a lonely old coot seeking a new lease on life. Now if you don't mind, I need to tend to my beloved wife."

"Harrold, stay with us just a little longer. The gravity of this situation is mind blowing. Someone or something's intending we bump into each other out here," Miranda speculated.

"Intriguing. Are either of you two ladies calling on a deceased soul tonight?"

"Yes, most definitely. My Jake was laid to rest at row thirty-nine, plot seven."

"Goodness, sorry for your loss, ma'am. My dear Alice nudges me to be infused with her forever. It's an overwhelming prospect, but exhilarating too. As long as my heart's healthy, I intend on fulfilling our plans. I lost her to cancer."

"How long ago?"

"Precisely *three years ago tonight*. Her suffering was bittersweet. We no longer reminisce in isolation. There are other persons laid to rest at Burkburnett waiting for absolution."

"So, Mr. Townsend, is there an unseen entity enabling you?"

"I believe so. She goes by the name Naomi. I'm her student now. She's teaching me so much about being in tune with Alice."

"In tune? What's that involve?"

"Instructing me to burn candles, hum melodies and cut myself in symbolic sacrifice. The stricter I obey, the nearer I feel to Alice. We read each another's minds. The dialogues and smooches are worth it all. And the darndest thing, lately I morph into a hot young bumblebee! She's quite the rose bush and sweet-talks me into pollinating her. We're fifty years younger!"

"*Bumblebee?*" Gretchen snickered. Hilarious expression, Mister! For the record, I'm a *bowl of peaches and cream* when I get transformed."

Gretchen felt everyone's blank stares.

"Okay, so much for attempting humor to break up this damn solemn occasion. Look peoples, I'm here to figure out why I'm being punished by the man who I never wanted to marry until this past week, when he showed up in my dreams looking like a male stripper. Most religions have a common conviction, that there's no sex in the next life, but I'm beginning to wonder. I mean, really, every time I see Jake he comes on to me. I need fucking answers!"

"Okay, I'll answer the riddle about the *Mender saying*," Harrold said. "The script's *love promise* is written into the moonlight."

"Huh? What guides me to Jake is wrapped around my neck and tucked under my blouse, see?"

"My word, what a beautiful gemstone that be!" Harrold said.

Gretchen scoffed and threw a hard glance at Miranda. "Alright, enough of the patronizing attitudes. I wanna talk to Naomi, the queen bitch herself. Can you two hook me up?"

Miranda contemplated. "It's up to Mr. Townsend to summon Naomi, since he's on better terms with her."

Harrold got all choked up. "I was simply wanting to speak with Alice tonight, not anything more. We'd be deviating from the standard rituals if a séance were performed."

"What harm could it do, now really?" Gretchen probed.

"In my psychic experiences, as long as we abstract information and not push the specters beyond their own nature, they'll be harmless and comply," Miranda surmised.

Harrold scowled. "Young woman, Alice Townsend's no damn ghost!"

"You're right, sir, my apologies."

"Keep an open mind, Mr. Townsend. Allow me to perform a purging of this place. The results might shock you."

Miranda took the Lepidolite crystal from her neck and rocked it hypnotically in front of the two.

"Any oppressive spirits be sent away from this sacred spot!" Miranda commanded.

Immediately, Gretchen's scarf changed into a golden circlet again. Harrold's altered into a silver sword. The handle donned a gallant lion's head with penetrating ruby eyes, one a medieval knight would proudly carry into battle.

"I'm quite impressed!" Harrold declared.

Harrold made a wish.

"Whoever's listening from the darkness, please allow my dear sweet Alice to appear tonight!"

Surprisingly, Harrold seared the tip of his sword over the candle flame, then scraped the blade across Alice's tombstone, mingling it with his own blood prints.

He pointed the lance toward the stars.

"Bow your heads in respect of the living and the dead. I bid the spirits to partake of this meeting."

Beads of nervous sweat puddled on their upper lips and eyebrows. The summer night breezes danced roundabout.

Without warning, several *Gatherer* creatures like Murtha, with spread dragon wings, plunged from the black sky, plundering neighboring gravesites. Their screeching and squealing sounds were hideous, almost too much to tolerate.

"Steady everyone," Harrold whispered. "Ignore those *flying creatures.*"

A dark reddish veil, pulsating with heavenly opulence, arose from Alice's plot. A central spherical orange capsule hummed like a vacuum, sucking in the tortured souls whose faint cries echoed from under the sod.

The silhouette of a fiery red-haired pagan goddess emerged from the muck.

Miranda extended her arm and pointed, "You're a demonic entity! Tell me your name, spirit! You're interfering with Harrold and Alice. I hereby cast you out of this place!"

"Hey, I know you!" Gretchen shrieked. "Go peddle your bling-bling somewhere else! This is the big leagues, bitch, and you're not welcomed here!"

She grabbed Harrold's sword and was about to charge the unkind spirit, but Harrold stopped her.

"So Naomi, this is your natural state? Gretchen chided. A hundred twenty-something years old, you say? You're a cunning sorceress, and the only one I blame for all the chaos!"

Aggravated, Naomi twirled her red dreadlocks with spindly fingers. She released a sinister giggle. The sound put shivers down their spines.

The ground shook as Naomi spoke.

"I'm an entity who flourishes in the *Mender Environment*, lightyears from here. I'm whimsical, a chameleon, appearing like a girl or old hag, depending on my mood. You and Harrold are blessed to interact with me. I channeled you to my *Habitat,* that ethereal paradise, to fellowship with your lovers. I've shaped how your minds and bodies anticipate irresistible urges; triggering the warmth and passionate sensations of reuniting, or constructing the dismal feelings upon separation to discourage you."

"Please Naomi, I can't bear further separation from Jake!" Gretchen whined. "Heartache sucks, if that's what you're implying. I feel like I'm trapped inside a game of Dungeons and Dragons."

A sickly sweet aroma flooded their nostrils.

"Man, that odor reminds me of the potion I guzzled at Jake's retreat. It tasted as good as it smelled..."

Miranda sensed an aberration and lowered the candle to earth level.

"Hey guys, pay attention! Things are crawling in the dirt!"

"Gretchen, you told Jake you wanted to '*discover an elixir which reignited your passion for life*,' so here it is," Naomi declared. "This graveyard's an aphrodisiac factory. The little insects underneath you are the *Dream Weavers*, makers of a delicious, juicy pick-me-up."

Naomi explained how the Bois d'Arc tree beetles scurry into the caskets, collect hair stems of deceased partners like Jake's, return above ground, where the Gatherers morph into owl entities and pluck living human hair to finish the recipe. White doves deliver the eternal qualities to the Mender Habitat to nourish partial spirits like Jake. Only the hair strands of true soul mates are woven together to form the scarfs. Droplets of blood are sorted into bottles and written onto the fabric to serve as homing beacons for lost paramours.

Spirit ripeness enables lost souls to perpetually remain youthful. Privileged lovers create a new world with their fiery passion, spawning

magnetic vibes which attract similar souls. When someone on earth desires his or her lost lover beyond the grave, the vibes cross through the
threshold of death and initiate a tender, instinctual response.

The *Ruffians* are part of a coven whose leader is *Stella the Diviner*. They
attempt to intercept the lovers' vibes by building a spiritual barricade
between the land of the living and the dead.

Naomi concluded her visit.

"I'm sending you back with an ample supply of my home-spun brew.
Go rescue a few lonely love birds in Saint Germaine, have them escorted
to Burkburnett. I impart potent gifts of seduction on you. Lure them
here to undertake the Hazing ritual. It's your rite of passage to become
a hot blooded *Virgin Temptress*, fully fuckable and utterly desired by that
sexy stud, Jake Conroe, who's waiting for you on the other side."

7

Naomi imbued Gretchen with mystic instincts. Jake was her catalyst, and she would sacrifice her entire essence for his affections.

A creature of the night, she tracked down wayward lovers to emancipate them from hopelessness. Her hunches were strong about matters of the heart.

The Blue Diamond bar on the outskirts of Saint Germaine, was her first testing ground.

As the sun was setting, Gretchen strolled nonchalantly into the establishment, attired in a floral sundress and sandals. She was seated at the far corner near the bathrooms, a great vantage point to observe the pack of partiers.

The pub was a jungle. A rock band was on stage setting up for the night's concert.

A *Ken and Barbie* type couple coasted into the scene, making their way to the watering hole. The twosome were a magnetic attraction for Gretchen.

Their auras are cloudy. I feel like such a voyeur wanting to know more.

"Load us up with some margaritas, heavy on the salt," the man demanded. "And my darling Abby has a special request."

"What might that be?" said the bartender.

"Um, we're celebrating our second anniversary. That Lemon Tart on your dessert menu is Abby's favorite happy ending."

"I'll get it right out, sir."

"No, on second thought, wait 'till we're ready to close out the tab, bad luck to mix sweets with alcohol."

"Ha ha, Ted you're such a goober, practicing self-control again?" Abby jabbed.

Ted and Abby chugged several rounds, but he wouldn't slow down.

"Goddamnit, Ted, you know what happens when we're tipsy."

Volatility ensued.

"Get lost!" Abby protested. She grabbed what remained of his drink and threw it on the floor.

The sounds of shattering glass echoed across the tavern.

Then came the shoving and cussing.

Gawking patrons circled like vultures, obstructing Gretchen's view from the falderal.

"I'm so done! All it takes is some teenage slut to make goo-goo eyes, then you drool like a horn dog!"

Abby stampeded toward the restroom, sobbing uncontrollably. Gretchen intervened as she passed by. "Let off some stress, sweetie. You're welcome to sit here for a while and chill."

Introductions were made. The tone was guarded but sincere. "I can't dawdle," said Abby. "Mark my words, he'll bolt over, flash those big brown puppy dog eyes, then apologize for flirting with that girl. I always take him back, so pathetic of me."

"Understood. But honestly, there's more going on here than meets the eye," Gretchen warned.

"You were watching us?" Abby suspiciously lashed back.

"Yes, in manner of speaking."

She jerked up, ready to leave.

"But it's not what you think, girl." Gretchen's arm gently lassoed Abby around the waist and sat her back down. "There...you might find my insights intriguing."

"I don't take kindly to stalkers, um, Miss Gretchen, or whatever your *real* name is…"

"I *am* real to a degree, but also deceivingly cunning, sorta like you."

"Pardon me?"

"Hear me out, honey. I can save you from future heartache."

"What heartache? Are you claiming to be a prophet?"

"Nah, I'm more like a *praying mantis* with a thousand eyes," Gretchen said.

Abby's face expressed confusion.

"May I call you Abby?"

"Abigail Gentry's the name, and yes, you have my permission."

"Thanks. So, my take on this, Abby, is that you did a great job of pinning blame on Ted, all the while that slim brunette guy was on your radar."

Abby threw Gretchen an angry glance.

"Ted's my fiancé, idiot. I have no clue who you're referring to."

"Abby, your dark blue, cloudy *aura* tells me otherwise. Your lack of trust and unhappiness can be treated though."

Abby looked back toward the bar, nervously scanning all the faces.

"…and I noticed your aura suddenly change to brilliant red. I felt your lustful vibes dance when that *other guy* walked through the door."

"What the fuck, Gretchen? It's obvious you and Ted are involved in a conspiracy to destroy me. Show me that *other guy*, where is he?"

Gretchen pointed to a section of the pub where the dart board players were congregating. "Watch the dude in the red tank top and curly long brown hair…"

Abby squinted, but couldn't lock on to the hypothetical figure. "Nice try, Gretchen."

"No, really. See, now he's tossing a dart…bullseye! That crescent moon tat with the initials *A.Z.* inscribed on his left shoulder's gorgeous art work, perhaps meant to commemorate someone very special?"

Abby's face turned white. She discharged a deeply guttural, foreboding laugh. "Um, Gretchen, who you just described was my *dead lover*, Zach!"

She slid down her blouse and camisole below the shoulder line, exposing flesh. "Unless you went tanning with me, there's no way in hell you would've known about our matching tattoos! Ted's tried umpteen times to get me to burn off the Z and replace it with a T."

Unexpectedly, the cell phone Abby was toting lit up like a Christmas tree. A violent vibrating and ringing started, triggered by an invisible source.

Tommie, Tommie, Tommie...

The incoming words flooded her screen.

"Goddamnit! This is my fourth replacement phone in as many months. That creeper's stalking me. I've changed cell plans, blocked it, even hired a detective and reported its behavior to the authorities, but it's indiscernible."

Gretchen grinded her teeth. Chills ran from her spine and to the bottoms of her feet, then shot back up to her head. A tingling sensation lingered.

"That *Tommie entity* trailing you, may not be a human at all. I know from experience. Three years ago at a camping trip, I blamed Jake for having an affair with somebody named *Tommie*, thinking *it* was a woman. I swore Jake was fucking *Tommie* behind my back. It was my anger that led to our breakup and his untimely accident. In my dreams Jake warned me to not play into its schemes. He suggested it's a *Ruffian* creature."

Abby showed a pensive streak.

"What's wrong, dear?" Gretchen probed.

"Well, that *Ruffian* thing's exploiting me. My stomach twists in knots when it starts provoking me..."

"About what, Abby?"

"Every few days it sends me pictures of some man's erect penis, chest and ass, but never its face, along with a ton of mushy poems and emojis. I'm helpless to stop the harassment. I've notified the police, but its network address is impossible to trace. They've never seen anything this stealthy before. It's even hacked into my online dating accounts, posing as a rich bachelor."

Gretchen paused in deep thought. "Girl, you and I must have some-thing in common that Tommie wants or needs...um, may I ask how Zach died?"

"He passed away on the operating table at Burkburnett General Hospital three years ago, after a freakish boating accident on Bois d' Arc Lake. A reckless boater collided with ours, and the propeller struck his head, cutting off his face. There were no witnesses except some old lady sitting in a rocking chair on the shore, smirking at me. No one's located her. It's as though she's vanished into thin air."

8

retchen's chance meeting with Abby at the Blue Diamond was monumental. To relish in their new friendship, she dispensed a small vial of Naomi's potion into Abby's frozen margarita to liven up the mood. They raised a toast to life, love and happiness. But the flames of desire to reunite with Jake and Zach remained unquenchable.

"Let's lose this crowd, break free from all conventional mindsets. Whatcha think of that?" Gretchen propositioned.

"Dang, you're some free-wheeling gypsy spirit, ready to conquer the world, Gretchen. Coincidentally, my drink tastes more like a root beer float than a margarita. I guess I'm losing my inhibitions...feelin' like soaring through puffy white clouds...let's go to my place for a nightcap. My townhouse is eight blocks away."

"Okay, but what will Ted think of you steppin' out on him? Isn't he already sensitive from tonight's episode?"

Abby chuckled. "He's been stroking his dick under the bar counter, fantasizing over that young blonde girl. He won't even notice I'm missing. I've already cut him off from getting any of my pussy, so I really can't blame him for his debauched ways."

"Sounds like some lyrics to a Country-Western song, Abby. But if you're good with it, then let's go!"

The girls exited the rear of the building. No street lights to guide them, only the occasional dog bark or cat fight to disrupt the stillness.

Naomi's liquid was starting to take effect. They behaved like giddy teenagers again. "What's happening to my body?" She inquired.

"I wanna let you in on a little secret," Gretchen responded. "When I go visit my Jake at the cemetery, I'm twenty years younger. I snuck a few droplets of that remedy into our drinks so you could sample it."

"You drugged me? That explains the change in taste," said Abby with astonishment.

"It's not dangerous. The stuff enhances our abilities to recognize the *living dead*. Besides, doesn't Zach deserve your best effort, Abby?"

"Absolutely, but why do I have to become a necromantic just to see him?"

"Abby, um, a more accurate rendition would be *falling for your soul mate in paradise*."

A commotion disrupted their chat.

A bat-like creature fluttered above the roof lines, picking off insects to snack on. Nimbly it changed altitude and dive-bombed Abby.

"Get out of here!" Abby screamed.

"Don't hurt it, that's a *Gatherer* with obvious intentions to get you closer to Zach!" Gretchen appealed.

Abby's arms flailed like a rag doll's...she ducked to avoid an impact... but too late, the bat-thing flapped around her head and tore out chunks of hair, then rose aloft.

In a show of aggression, a *Ruffian* intercepted the Gatherer in midair. Claws were drawn, as the two entities scuffled, rolling up into an angry ball, like two boa constrictors trying to suffocate each other.

A prize was at stake.

"Abby, you're witnessing a supernatural struggle for supremacy."

"Over a dyed piece of my hair? You've gotta be kidding!" Abby ranted sarcastically, as she patted her scalp to check for injuries.

"It isn't that simple. Unwittingly, you've been transmitting out deliciously sensuous frequencies tonight. Zach's effigy at Blue Diamond probably rekindled your imagination to pursue his affections. Naomi from the Mender Habitat, and Stella the Diviner simultaneously received your harmonic intentions, and dispatched their agents here—one to *bless*, and the other to *block* you."

Abby's cell phone rang. "Did someone just butt dial me?" She grasped the cell in her rear jean pocket to view an incoming message, 'Celebrate newness of life. MENDERS will guide to your dead lover's heartbeat.'

She was delirious with confusion.

The moment Abby repeated the phrase in a mumbled, low-pitched voice, the Gatherer and Ruffian disappeared into the blackness.

"Your guess is as good as mine, Abby, as to which one of those birds of prey stole your hair."

Immediately, Abby saw another message come through. "Hey, Gretchen, Tommie sent me a link to an unknown website. Should I click on it?"

"This is where things get complex. I suspect Naomi *and* Stella are using that *Tommie entity* as an avatar to get to us. Go ahead, open the web address, I'm curious as fuck who's playing us."

Abby warily opened the link. It initiated a download to her phone. Ghosts in the machine.

"Oh my God, it's a video of my dead lover, Zachary Branum!" she shrieked. "He's blowing me a kiss in the fog!"

"Abby, my phone's buzzing too! It's Jake! He's doing the same damn thing!"

"Ha ha! It gets better, Gretchen..."

"Whatcha mean?"

"They're in a familiar setting... I'm getting a GPS map popping up....wait, it's giving us the coordinates to....a location 1.2 miles from where we're standing...it's my street! *Right now* they're kicking back in the basement of Meadow Creek Village. It's the site of our fitness club in the downstairs basement! They wanna hook up!"

9

Gretchen and Abby acted like cottontail does in heat, sprinting through the backstreets of Saint Germaine, searching for their elusive bucks.

The two hot messes entered the trendy four story Meadow Creek Village complex. To prepare for the naughty encounter, Gretchen dabbed on fresh lipstick and retouches of makeup, while Abby brushed her curls and chomped on some minty gum. Abby chipped her fingernail while poking frantically at the elevator button.

A time capsule of dreams.

The elevator was a portal, transitioning them into a sphere where tender breezes played with their hair. Gravity was twice that of earth. The landscape was blanketed in an amber twilight, where lovers could count the stars while the sun still shined through the euphoric haze. The planet Saturn was visible in the sky, along with three crescent shaped moons.

The girls were stunned.

They stood on a white marble deck overlooking a vast, calm sea inlet. A variety of sea life flourished. The tide pools at the edge of the shoreline were extraterrestrial hot tubs generating an unknown source of heat. Emerald, ruby, sapphire and diamonds were latticed together in spectacular patterns to form them. Provocative aromas of Lavender, Jasmine, Patchouli, Sandalwood, Sweet Orange and Ylang Ylang inundated their nostrils.

They turned slack jaw, as the form of a half-man, half-woman approached.

"Welcome special guests Abigail Gentry and Gretchen Lanners, to the Mender Retreat," the entity announced.

"Whoa! Hello there, Murtha!" Gretchen exclaimed. "Last time I saw you, I was with Jake at that mountain hideaway, remember? And this here is my new friend Abby..."

Murtha grinned.

"Damn, Gretchen, we're celebrities!" Abby boasted.

Murtha the Mender bowed genteelly. "Make yourselves comfortable and stay awhile."

At the changing station, they swapped out their street clothes for beautiful silk bath robes. Murtha pointed them toward the ocean stairway which led to the hot tub tide pools.

Jake and Zach were reclining in the VIP section, each humming their lady's favorite love song.

"Aw, how sentimental! I guess this is our invitation to get *really* wet," said Gretchen.

They giggled with glee at the thought of having tide pool sex with their god-like lovers.

About to disrobe and step into the water, a new voice tantalized them. "Not so fast, ladies, I'm Darcy the Mender Healer. You two are scheduled for a body rub to relax those tight muscles. Your suitors over there aren't going anywhere. In fact, they're the ones who insist on *full* body treatments."

Darcy focused her mind with a blank stare at the ground.

The beach scenery shifted around in front of them. A platform with two massage tables arose from under the sand. A telescoping object with imitation palm fronds fanned out to provide shade.

Darcy escorted them to the tables and advised they disrobe and lay down on their stomachs.

"Holy fuck! Look at us!" Abby screamed with joy. "These changes to my body are surreal! I never want to go back to Saint Germaine!"

Ambient classical music wafted in from all around. Jake and Zach squeezed out some ointment from silver tubes and caressed the girls' backs and glutes.

Abby couldn't restrain her emotions once she felt Zach's loving touch. She turned around and pulled him toward her. She stroked his face and brushed her trembling hands across his chest and torso. "Sweetheart, your head doesn't bleed anymore! You got your face back! I won't ask how all this happened, I'm just grateful to be in your presence again."

The guys performed fetish foot worship. Their hard dicks were strategically cupped within the souls of the girls' feet, gyrating their hips and probing the women's pussy lips with their forked tongues, tapping the clits with expert precision.

Gretchen and Abby fizzed with gratification and begged for more stimulation. They gladly flipped over like buttery pancakes on a sizzling griddle, legs spread wide open, offering up more of themselves. They drenched them with feathery touches and sweetly kissed their bellybuttons, following the tiny forest of body hair, that enticing treasure trail, down to the honey pot. Their legs shivered and shook with every stroke of their lovers' flicking tongues while they climaxed multiple times.

"Hey, boss man! It's time for some role switching," Gretchen said seductively.

"What do you have in mind, sexy thang? You cowgirls wanna slip into those stirrups and ride these wild stallions?" Jake irresistibly suggested.

Zach expressed soothing intonations. "Abby, my love, I'm pleased you had the faith to follow Gretchen here from Saint Germaine. That was me at the Blue Diamond pub throwing darts. Even though I was undetectable to you, I still turned around and shot some cupid arrows in your direction!"

Abby was elated. "Zach, now that you mention it, I did feel puffs of displaced air hit me. I would walk over hot glass embers to see you again.

Fortunately, Gretchen's been acting as our medium...the last few years have been stifling without you."

"Okay, love birds, refocus!" Jake poked. "You gals said you wanted to do something kinky together, right? Well, here's your chance. See those steamy baths over there?"

The girls quivered.

"Really? Whatcha' hiding inside them, Jake? Can't you see we're horny?" Gretchen squealed.

The dudes stood up and strutted over to the foamy froth, showing off their manly hardware. Those donkey dicks, low-hanging balls and rock-hard asses were a sight to savor.

Abby rejoiced. "Just what the doctor ordered, Gretchen! Who's gonna go first?"

The girls raced several feet and cannonballed into the water, soaking the men with huge splashes; their bodies sinking downward into the oxygen-laden, effervescent bubbles. They squirmed to fight off the rip tide. It pulled them under...the more they thrashed and kicked, the deeper into the abyss they drifted, never to resurface.

10

esieged by Romeo's doggie slobber, Gretchen awoke in her bed all panicky.

"Help me! I'm fuckin' drowning! I'm too damn young to die!"

Sister Callie tugged at Romeo's collar to stop him from licking Gretchen's face.

"Chill out, I'm here for you." Callie dabbed a cold washcloth on sis's forehead and reshuffled the pillows to make her comfortable.

"Where's Jake and Zach? They promised us a revelation if we entered the tide pools with them! Fuck it, in typical fickle fashion, they wimped out again!"

"Um, Gretchen, who is 'They?' Please enlighten me. I'm trying to be a good sister, but you're on the verge of having a relapse. You've been absent from your job for over two days.   Luckily, I called your boss Joe and said you're out with the flu. This partying around Saint Germaine has to end. A couple of my friends saw you stumble out of a bar downtown with some unknown woman. Seems like you're backsliding into your old habits again."

"Pardon me? Then why'd you bother to come over and rescue me if I'm such a burden, Callie? You'll always be my big sister, but I have an ancient soul, so stop the bitching and attempt a little compassion."

"Get to the point, Gretch. What far-fetched fantasy have you been reminiscing over?"

"Hey, enough Callie! Your cynical attitude isn't helping me recover. I just returned from an incredibly romantic place with Jake and some friends. That elevator portal and hot tub were dope as hell. Naomi's a creative genius, so I don't appreciate you trying to steal my joy."

"Show me some proof you're not falling into a delirium, Gretch. That's all I ask and I'll back off."

"You've already seen glimpses of Jake's presence running amuck in my house. You uncovered that picture frame in my guest bedroom a couple of nights ago, which captured Jake's grimacing dead face in the casket, smeared with Egyptian red rouge, the color I never wear."

"So what? Anybody can Photoshop a picture. You have to be more convincing than that to sway my opinion, Gretch."

"Then how about Jake's cologne being tampered with, and my head injury? Hell, my bedroom closet's a passage to the Mender Habitat. Romeo went with me to visit Jake."

"Face the music, sis, you haven't left this house for days. Let's move to the kitchen so I can pour you a sudsy Black and Tan to change up this bad mood," Callie pleaded.

Gretchen grinned. "A peace offering would do us good...besides, I miss chatting with my best friend and not arguing anymore."

"Then do me a favor, girl, and get dressed. You have a bad habit of sleeping in the buff..."

"Huh?"

She stood up from the bed. The blanket fell to her feet, revealing her sunburned body.

A gaudy sparkle on Gretchen's navel almost blinded Callie.

"Holy shit, is that what I think it is, Gretch? A belly button ring and stone?"

"Uh, I don't have a clue how that got there..."

"Let me inspect your body, maybe it's gonna give up some more secrets of your bad behavior."

Callie turned her around like a rotisserie chicken, looking for extra markings.

"Bingo! In addition to the new tummy ring and sunburn, which I suspect is due to skinny dipping, I see two red bruises on your neck. Let me guess, you're gonna blame Romeo for those hickeys."

Gretchen jerked the mirror from the bed stand and inspected herself.

"Wow! So this is what Jake meant when he promised me a surprise. I wonder if Zach gave Abby a similar reward."

Gretchen's back and forth texting with Abby spiraled into frenetic Hyena-like chortling.

"Stop the texting, Gretch! Those clicking and guttural noises are annoying as hell. Let's have some sisterly time like we discussed."

"But you'll love Abby's discovery! She has the exact piercing and markings on her skin! She did some quick homework and texted these pics as proof! Our skin blemishes are actually body art. One's the symbol of a chalice, and the other's a Mender dove. And the mysterious little green stone attached to my belly ring? It's a rare but potent piece of *Moldavite* crystal, according to Abby's research."

"Intriguing. You might make me a believer after all," Callie said. "Just slip on your robe. I might be ready to listen to your exotic travels and escapades; a few strong drinks should get our sibling friendship back on track."

11

The girls moved to the kitchen. Callie made refreshing night-
caps. Gretchen glanced at Romeo and noticed he was wearing
a red scarf and grappling a big bone in his jowls.

"Put that horrid thing down, Romeo! You're drooling everywhere!"
Gretchen commanded. "I thought I disposed of that rotten thing days
ago." She inspected Romeo closer. "And where'd you get that red bandana, doggie? Um, you haven't been back to see Jake without me, have
you?"

Romeo's ears twitched, as though he understood what was said. He
released the bone from his mouth. The brash sound of it ricocheting off
the floor startled them.

Even more, it gave up secrets.

"Looky there!" Gretchen squealed. "There's a small hinge on the
ball joint that's popped open. Do you think they're loose pins from
some reconstructive surgery?"

Callie reacted. "I'm no forensic anthropologist, Gretch, but it does
look odd. Pins would mean it's been a part of some laboratory experi-
ment where the rest of the body's gone missing..."

Gretchen futzed with it.

"This damn thing's been drilled out and made hollow! And there's a slice of parchment paper rolled up inside!"

Carefully she tugged on the tablet. It had a unique leathery consistency and crackled as it came in contact with room temperature. The girls' eyes were saucer-like as Gretchen pressed it down on the table top.

"What the hell are those hieroglyphic-like symbols?" Callie asked. "It's all gibberish to me!"

They took a few swigs of ale and kept inspecting it.

"I think I got this! My psychic buddy Miranda taught me a few things about deciphering maps and shit."

Without hesitation, Gretchen untied her robe and unclipped the Moldavite ring from her tummy. She held the green crystal in her fingers while scanning the cryptic manuscript top to bottom.

"Ta-da! Callie, take a listen to this prose!" Gretchen mused.

Clear words exploded onto the page. She read them aloud to Callie:

— ∼

My sweet Gretchen,

Hope this scroll reaches you safely, thanks to your pooch Romeo. I sent him through the Mender portal, where he retrieved this message. Sorry I had to use such a gruesome chew toy to camouflage it, but we can't risk being detected by the wrong set of eyes, now that Stella's psychic forces are tracking you.

Her malicious energy is disturbing our love affair. Lately when you travel through a passageway to be with me, we get sabotaged.

Naomi constantly warns us to beware of Stella the Diviner and her Ruffian drones! They're hijacking love frequencies in hyperspace. We're most vulnerable to their attacks during intense foreplay or while transitioning between worlds. The first moment we met at Burkburnett, I

noticed them hanging out like schoolyard bullies, looking to exploit grief sick lovers. Since then you've grown
in spirit ripeness, which attracts them even more.

You hit your head and fell unconscious in the hot tub.
We pulled you out, but not before Stella's incantation
was cast on you and Abby. Naomi helped me attach a
Moldavite piercing onto your tummy for protection and
discernment. Yours and Abby's new body art wasn't
fashioned by Naomi. We believe them to be sophisticated
tracking devices installed by Stella to obsess over you two.
One of her Ruffians already infested Abby's and your cell
phones, remember?

Naomi says she's proud you're showing good progress toward spirit ripeness. For us to achieve complete unity,
you'll soon need to return to Burkburnett Cemetery to
complete the Virgin Hazing.

Stella's kingdom is for the disenchanted. Her cruel
Ruffian squad mimic forlorn lovers, but inflict moods
of shame, depression and desperation to block good intentions. Anybody who gets ensnared by Stella's trickery
will be forever isolated from ecstasy.

Consider this letter as a friendly reminder to pursue these
Symbols of Transformation. The skills acquired will
thwart Stella's attempts to lead you astray. Remember,
the Mender world is all about the dead and living coming
together in paradise, celebrating soul mate love:

Bois d'Arc Beetles and Dream-weaving Doves –
Encourage them always to deliver strands of hair to our
habitat so our followers grow in number.

Designer Scarfs – Transforms any believer into youthful, hot blooded radiance!

Chalice energy drinks – Gulp down some home brew
and lose your inhibitions!

Clarity Crystals – Lepidolite and Moldavite stones unleash fourth- dimension consciousness.
Paradise Dating – Maintain love freshness with trips to
erotic destinations!
Matchmaker recruiting – Assist Naomi in recruiting
similar romantic species.
Soul mate enlightenment – Learn to gaze into my soul
while making love.
THE VIRGIN HAZING *– To save a Mender princess
from her plight.
* Not for the faint of heart

Babe, be watchful of returning dreams, as they harbor
our destiny. I hope we cross paths again soon. Cheers to
our eternal love!
Jake Conroe
Xoxo

Callie grabbed the docket so tersely it almost ripped. "This still looks
like a bunch of garbled shit to me. The composition sounds like a hyped
up travel brochure you need 3-D glasses to understand."

Gretchen shook her head in frustration. "I'm not pretending, I swear!
It's the real deal, and if you're wondering, I'm not on any meds either."

"Um, well just explain to me why these past few weeks you've been all
obsessed with Jake. When he was living, you never once declared your
devotion to him. You even told me he was at the top of your *playbook*, that
list of dudes notched on your belt. Now all of a sudden, you're acting
like a bereaved spouse who's lost her lover boy. Besides, he was consider-
ably older, and could have been your father. For once please be transparent with me; as the sister who raised you, I deserve a little insight into
how your mind works, don't I?"

"Alright, sis. I'll make an effort to clarify some things for the sake
of our relationship."

In a rare gesture of tenderness, Gretchen extended her arms across the table and held her sister's hands, stroking the tops lightly with her thumbs.

"Sure Jake's older than me, but he's taught me a lot about life lately. When he was mortal, things were different between us."

"How so?"

"He kept insisting we marry. 'Third time's a charm,' he would always say. If I remember accurately, he popped the question a hundred times a day, at least that's how it felt. He bombarded me with such intensity, it counteracted any chance we might have had to settle down together."

"Didn't a clever sage once say, 'Love is Love' Gretch? We're not supposed to resist the natural order of things."

"Perhaps, but true love doesn't demand I forsake my own identity just to be his muse."

"Well, Gretch, you know Mom and Dad loved Jake. On Saturdays, he would drive over four hours from East Texas to reach Houston, weaving through the back roads just to be at our house before sunrise. I looked on in jealousy when he made a wicked batch of hot chocolate, which he brought to your bedside, along with those single red rose stems."

The girls giggled, but all the reminiscing began to take its toll on Gretchen.

"Look, before I met Jake in his new body, I refused to be a cliché, a sexy bride dancing to sour love songs, surrounded by miserable people, themselves stuck in unfulfilled relationships. Since Naomi's improved my figure, now I have Jake back in my arms whenever the mood's right. We have a hassle-free relationship with all the perks, no more synthetic love."

"Girl, you're still in the land of us humanoids. You haven't departed this life, at least not in the physical sense. You spin saucy tales of forbidden soirees, as though Jake's your rogue knight and you hold court at Camelot. Are you trying to conceal the darker aspects of the relationship? Not sure which way you guys are leaning."

"That's bullshit!" Gretchen protested. "I'm not his whore, and he's not my gigolo, if that's what you're implying. He's obviously selling his entire soul just to be with me again from across the Great Beyond. The only bummer is what Jake wrote in that scroll. I have to reach the next level if I ever want to revert back permanently to my youthful appearance and claim a place next to him as his elite lover and bed warmer."

"Do you think your sorceress friend Naomi will allow me to meet Jake, if what you say is true?"

"I think that can be arranged, Callie. Let me reach out to Jake and see."

12

Callie sat back as the silent observer, while Gretchen readied her cell phone to connect with Jake.

Initiating communication through electronic components was risky business; the Ruffians were constantly meddling with their digital love frequencies, hampering intimacy by injecting supernatural Trojan viruses and Ruffian malware into the airwaves.

Gretchen's doorbell rang. It was Abby.

"Hey, girl, it's great to see you so soon after our trip to the tide pools."

"Didn't you summon me here tonight, Gretch?"

"Um, what do you mean?"

Abby showed her a text. It had come from Gretchen's phone.

Gretchen was alarmed. "That's impossible, my cell's been recharging all night! Follow me to the kitchen and meet my older sister Callie, she'll vouch for me."

Abby and Callie shook hands and made small talk.

"Here goes nothing, girls. I'm gonna prove to Abby I never sent her a text tonight. Cross your fingers and say a little prayer while I turn this beastie on."

Frenetic images of a female form with jet black dreadlocks scrolled across her screen. She was an ominous creature with penetrating emerald eyes, bare chested with nipple ring piercings. She gripped a glowing torch and stood under a cavernous archway made of white frosted crystalline quartz, symbolic of deception entrapped in ice.

A tattoo of a slithering rattlesnake with a skull head ran from her lower stomach and in between her breasts. The reptile's forked tongue split in two and curled back around to form a heart shape on her neck. Her sultry voice was almost inaudible.

The scratchy words, 'I am Stella, join my virgin brothel, and I'll change you into a sexy Playboy Bunny, where you'll get all the dick you want!' were aired, along with strange texting symbols.

Gretchen fussed. "So that's what Stella the Diviner looks like! She's definitely a catty hoe and is intent on recruiting me. Hell, I never want to meet her in a dark alley, she's spooky as fuck!"

She was close to turning off the gadget when the inexplicable feminine entity vanished.

Then eerie silence.

A digitized voice similar to Siri broadcasted a message. 'Mender encrypted security session has commenced. This transmission is now completely hack-proof. Stella and her Ruffians are no longer capable of infecting your phone. Thank you for your patience and have a lovely day.'

Gretchen was caught off guard and almost dropped the phone.

A real time video of Jake reclining on the deck of a huge yacht popped up. The picture panned left to reveal Zach. Both were wearing sunglasses and spreading suntan lotion on their hard, rippling abs, biceps and chests. They called out the girls' names and blew synchronized kisses at them. The soothing sound of the ocean breezes and rhythmic pounding of the tide upon the shoreline made the girls flustered.

Gretchen and Abby squealed like frenzied coyotes at the thought of meeting up, but Callie was vexed.

"Oh Jake, my love," Gretchen begged, "do me a favor before our transmission gets distorted, and shout out to my sister here. She's still unconvinced that you're alive and well out there. "

"For sure. Testing one, two three. Can you hear and see me, Callie?

She nodded.

"So, it feels like forever since we've talked, Callie. I apologize for the shock of all this."

Callie was sheepish. "You look really good, Jake, at least from the vantage point of this camera lens thingy. Congratulations for the turn-around. I only seek Gretchen's happiness. Please promise me you'll protect her while she's occupied with you. Your interplanetary romps are making her get in trouble at work. I don't want her to get fired, okay?"

"Not a problem, Callie. Just be open minded."

She was skeptical. "Uh, what are you suggesting?"

"See, we reserved this sixty-foot yacht for the weekend and want to transport the girls here as soon as possible to get the party started. You and Romeo are invited, but that's up to you."

She shook her head. "No, I'm good. I have to watch this place and take care of Romeo. What you wrote Gretchen in that letter leads me to believe she and Abby are in imminent danger from Stella and her Ruffian crew. How can you guarantee their safety? Besides, I don't want to explain their disappearance to our family and friends if they decide to stay with you and not return home to Saint Germaine."

"Your concerns have merit, but I have the perfect solution. Poke around inside that chew toy. There's another compartment which holds your answer."

Shots of adrenaline coursed through the girls' bodies. Abby held one end of the bone while Callie wedged her fingers inside. She dislodged the object. A beautiful, Brazilian amethyst geode rolled out.

Callie looked disgusted. "So Jake, you're trying to earn my trust by giving me a crusty old piece of rock?"

"No, Callie. It's much more than that."

He snapped his fingers. The sound projected through the airwaves. The precious stone lit up like a crystal ball. "See? It functions as an omnipresent video surveillance system. As long as you two wear those Moldavite belly button piercings, which act as micro antennas riding on the Mender terrestrial frequencies, you're free to chase your indiscretions. Callie can keep an eye on y'all but at a distance!"

Callie gave in to Jake's logic.

Abby and Gretchen couldn't contain themselves, dancing all over the kitchen like rebels on the prowl, while Romeo launched some cheerful barks.

"Just one more order of business before we prep you girls for a trip to our ocean paradise."

"Fetch the scarf, Gretch. Remember, it's of Mender origin, high on the list of supreme tools for transformation."

Gretchen held one end of the scarf, while Abby firmly latched on to the other end. He recited a chant and the original scarf subdivided into two scarfs.

He asked them to dab a section directly onto their necks where Stella's embedded homing apparatuses were situated. Before their eyes, the ingenious fabric functioned as a supernatural antibiotic which healed and beautified their skin.

"There you go! Stella's helpless to tamper with you two anymore! Shame on her for injecting imitation Mender symbols into your sacred epidermis!"

The girls were elated with their clean bill of health.

"Y'all ready to come party with us?"

"Hell yeah!" they chirped.

"Sweet, now for some bad ass indulgence...come and reclaim your macho men. We're waiting for ya!"

13

Gretchen's house was the only one in her neighborhood under the siege of thunder and lightning. Gale force winds whipped around like a tornado, followed by torrential rains. All the lights and appliances flickered off and on.

"A helluva way for Naomi to get our attention," Gretchen murmured to Abby.

Callie and Romeo fell into a trance and were frozen in time, unmovable as though under the influence of a hibernating spell.

The deluge broke through the rafters. The flash flood consisted of a substance similar to mercury, stopping just a few inches from their heads.

The girls felt the urge to be young again.

The molten elements were a magnetic canopy, deliberately tugging their revitalized feminine bodies down the hallway. They lurched toward the garage door, the gateway to Jake and Zach's world.

An oasis of anticipation.

The doorframe changed into a set of lofty marble Corinthian pillars, luring their curiosities into the deep thicket which lay ahead. They crossed through an expansive, magnificent royal garden which was flush with perfectly maintained rose bushes, flowers and shrubs. The centerpiece was a grand fountain the shape of a mermaid with jets of water spewing from her nipples.

Numerous tropical birds, peacocks and dancing swans occupied the sanctuary. They formed a chorus of titillating noises. Turtledoves were roosting and cooing in the adjoining pine grove. A pearly sandy substance soaked into their bare feet, a tactile treat to ease their stresses from the trek.

A euphoric voice from somewhere said, "Leave your fears behind and wade out into the fountain!"

They shot into the pond without reservation, giggling and tussling around. Abby started a water fight and splashed Gretchen.

An invisible tide rolled in. They treaded water to stay afloat, but a huge wave crashed over and dragged them under the surface.

The next minute their heads bobbed up into a watery dimension which spawned a new awareness. The seagulls hovering overhead meant land was near. They floated in the salty ocean as two castaways looking for a rescue boat. Instead, a pair of platinum colored dolphins with saddles and straps trilled and flipped their tails in friendly mannerisms, inviting Gretchen and Abby to mount them.

They rode through a Sargasso Sea, zig zagging between coral reefs and rocky shoreline until arriving at a secluded cove. Tethered to golden buoys were several huge yachts anchored in the harbor.

The dolphins squirted a stream of rainbow colored water from their blowholes to announce the girls' arrival. The commotion caught the attention of Jake and Zach, who were sunning themselves on the bow of their vessel.

"Ahoy Mateys!" Zach yelled. "It be ye lucky day, come hang out wit' us!"

The dolphins shimmied up to the boat, while the guys hoisted down the ladder. When the girls arrived on deck, Jake and Zach planted such intense kisses on their lips, bolts of electricity spiked into the air. Their mutual affection lasted an eternity, the way it should be dispensed by those who're madly in love.

"How opulent! So this is how you two dudes live when we're apart," Abby snorted.

"Sort of. It's just as lonely here as it is back on earth when you're not sharing these panoramas with us," Jake said. "Notice we're docked in the shape of a circle along with other boats? At tonight's bonfire you'll meet some inspirational guests and crew here at the Mender port. It'll blow your mind how the evening will unfold!"

Zach pointed toward the coastline. "See...just past the jetty...there's the hot tub tide pools and shady cabana you two enjoyed during your last stay."

"Whoa, I wondered why it all looked familiar, but the passageway we took this time to get here was a totally new experience. Those dolphins were dope," Gretchen beamed.

Jake motioned for everyone to go below deck for a tour.

"...and over here's our seafaring bungalows designed to rejuvenate wayward travelers. Before this vacation concludes, you two'll be well acquainted with our supply of spiced pirate rum and the spaciousness of the captain's chambers where our love will be constantly consummated."

The girls' inclinations prodded them to rip off Jake and Zach's speedos and perform blow jobs on the spot.

Gretchen and Abby dug their fingernails into the sex gods' butt cheeks and sucked their dicks so dry, as though trying to dislodge hidden diamonds from the bottom of their ball sacks.

The phenomenal sexual release left the dudes breathless and speechless; their celestial bodies slumped on the cabin bed like two big cats who'd just finished mating with their lionesses on the Serengeti.

While the guys were napping, the girls plundered the liquor cabinet. Jugs of eighteenth century Bordeaux and Scotch shimmered in alcoholic glory, awaiting their taste buds.

The girls didn't resist the opportunity to get wasted.

"To hell with the fancy sauce, where's the goddamn spiced rum, the kind I loved to guzzle out on Bois d'Arc lake where Jake and I used to camp?"

"Tear the room apart, that keg Jake mentioned is hiding here somewhere!" Abby blurted.

Gretchen uncovered an old oak chest sitting inside a baroque style marble armoire.

"Hey, lookie here, Abby! The locket's unlatched. Check out all the gold doubloons!"

The girls' faces shown greediness as they pilfered the forbidden treasure.

"Where do we spend all this loot? I didn't spot a Sachs or Neiman's anywhere on this island," Abby complained.

"Err, tell me about it girl! Do you think we can stash them in our purses and bring the booty back through the portal?" Gretchen suggested.

Abby rolled off an explosive laugh. "Hey chic, we're wearing bikinis and no other accessories. Besides, no one up here seems to disclose where that damn worm hole might be located on this island. Last time it formed at the Mender tide pools."

At closer inspection, they noticed strange symbols imprinted on the currency. Some had images of flying doves, others were of goblets, owls and dolphins. But one especially stood out. It was in the likeness of a beautiful long haired maiden, thrusting a sword into an object the shape of a human heart. The flip side of the coin contained the phrase, '*Cast ye Virgin into th' frothy mirth 'n make ye way to shore.*'

"Now that's one hell of a provocative phrase!" Gretchen blared. "Any translators familiar with pirate blabber on board?"

14

The setting sun, pierced by a mythological archer's arrow, spilled forth a sleepy brim of orange dusk over the Mender harbor.

The girls had been snoozing off a bad hangover for hours, while their men were busy spear fishing near the barrier reef. They awoke to the smoky aroma of a huge bonfire on the beach. The faint outline of several human forms scurrying about the shoreline caught their attention.

"I'm assuming those persons over there came from these group of yachts? Strange we hadn't spotted one soul in this harbor until now," said Gretchen. "It's almost as though they were staged by some higher power to enter this place at the precise time we woke up."

"Chill, Gretch. While you've been snoozing, I've done some detective work. The phrase on these bizarre coins, *'Cast ye Virgin into th' frothy mirth 'n make ye way to shore,'* might be our chance to get to the coast without having to swim."

"Huh?"

"Here, take this," Abby instructed. She handed Gretchen one of the Virgin gold coins. "Follow me up to the top deck, we're gonna try getting these to skip as far toward the beach as possible."

The girls took deep breaths and stretched out their arms like a pitcher to warm up. The Virgin coins were pinched between their fingers, squarely aligned with the rolling surf; once released, both golden objects skimmed the water and hopped over and over as though self-propelled. Each time they made impact, a stepping stone pathway began forming several inches above the waves.

Gretchen was delighted. "I'll be damned! We can easily navigate these cobblestones all the way to the bonfire! Zach and Jake will be amused when they find out we're one step ahead of them."

"Let's at least show some courtesy by leaving a note behind telling them where we've gone!" Abby insisted.

Both were engaged in uproarious laughter until their bellies hurt.

By the time they hopscotched over the watery rock pathway to the beachfront, a crowd of beings had clustered to greet them.

Murtha the Mender Gatekeeper strolled up.

"May your time spent at the Mender fire ceremony be fulfilling and ease your spirits," Murtha declared. "Might I introduce you to our other guests? Do not be alarmed, for they represent *soul mate unions* from every corner of your beloved earth, going back in history several millennia."

"Uh, sure thing," Gretchen said skeptically.

"So when are our sexy boss men gonna return from their fishing expedition?" Abby inquired.

"I'm sure very soon, Ma'am," Murtha reassured.

At the center of the pyre was a portal where the silhouettes of several eccentric couples emerged. As the ushers guided them toward the seating, they held hands and showed platonic affection for one another.

"Oh holy shit! Harrold, is that you?" Gretchen screamed.

"Yes, dear. A few nights after I met you and Miranda at Burkburnett, my beloved Alice called me home for good. Alice, it's my pleasure to introduce Gretchen Lanners to you."

Alice smiled. Her eyes shown through to her soul. Her green aura was soaked with charm and calming vibes.

"Your bride looks so beautiful!" Abby said. "How old are you two, pushing twenty-three?"

Harrold and Alice broke out into chuckles.

Other couples were idling in the shadows waiting to make their acquaintance.

"When Jake died, I started chugging tequila from an empty soda bottle, and would sit on the park bench, watching all the lonely people walking their dogs. Maybe they weren't the lonely ones after all. I was the one ready to give up, even though I had so much male attention. I realized way too late that only in Jake's presence was I fulfilled. The loneliness I felt was really an inner yearning to be back with him."

Gretchen's reminiscent mood stirred the gathering. They hungered for more.

"I sat back for years and took Jake's affections for granted. He was the only man who made love to me with every dimension of his soul. Let's get real people, a woman should discern the difference between a boy-toy and a rarified, mature lover. Jake would lock his eyes on me and treat me like fresh fallen snow, when he could've easily been seduced by all the scantily clad hotties. I distracted every inch of him. That's true love. I simply fucked up and ignored the best thing that ever happened to me, until Naomi reconnected us at the cemetery."

The people clapped and cheered to her story.

A man and woman oozing with the air of nobility approached. The lady gave Gretchen a sustained hug. "My name is Isabella Maestas, Countess of Catalonia," she said proudly. "And this distinguished gentleman standing next to me is my ancient lover, Prince Rinaldo."

Everyone but Gretchen and Abby curtsied to show respect for the royal couple.

"What do you mean by *ancient lover*?" Abby asked.

"As it sounds, m'Lady," the Countess replied, "Rinaldo is my Spanish knight. We were introduced by a mutual courtier many centuries before you were born."

"Amazing!" Gretchen yelled. "Tell me how you sovereigns stumbled on this playground in the sky."

"M'Lady, I was sent to the gallows due to false allegations arising from my love *for him*. A jealous baron from the Royal Court schemed and swore on his honor that I was Rinaldo's mistress. Contrary to his claims, I am in fact, Rinaldo's true betrothed, his *virgin in waiting*."

Rinaldo spoke. "Due to Naomi's great and tender mercies, the Countess returned to me in this afterlife. My persistent prayers over time convinced Naomi to grant me to partake in her Virgin Hazing and save us from eternal separation."

"That's bad ass, Sir Rinaldo, or whatever you go by!" Gretchen yelped. "I guess we have to bow and kiss your hand to pay homage."

Rinaldo smiled and edged over to Gretchen. "Madam," he proclaimed. "This splendid kingdom is a royal ossuary. Those sufferable yet penitent souls who have yearned for reunification over a lost lover are redirected here. 'Tis my hope for your sake, that your afflictions are mitigated, and that your spirit soars with Jake in eternity."

"Well thank you for the sweet blessing, sir!" Gretchen bowed in respect. "But how do you know my Jake Conroe?"

"Yes, as to your fitting question, in this realm we all partake of the seeds of eternal youth and fellowship. We are driven as one community, where no bereaved soul is isolated. The earth, from whence you came, is so vile..."

The crowd began to chant otherworldly hymns of happiness. Murtha instructed everyone to have a seat around the bonfire so the night's festivities could commence.

Several Gatherer and Mender creatures swooped in, feeding large cedar logs harvested from the Mender forests into the swelling campfire. The emanating heat parched Gretchen and Abby's throats. Their supple foreheads dripped with beads of perspiration.

A human form appeared in the center of the roaring flames. Everyone's necks strained to catch a glimpse of the entity.

The figure was Naomi. She was holding on to an old chest.

"I've invited some displaced ghosts who occupy this sealed box. By breaking the locket with my sword, each essence will be liberated in succession to provide you some entertainment and prove there are other dimensions operating right under your noses."

"Discharge the ghosts!" The crowd yelled.

"Exercise patience," said Naomi.

She raised an ivory sword to eye level and mightily thrust against the lock.

The blunt force broke it open.

Naomi warily unfastened and opened the lid. *'Doce nos vero antiqui manes!'* (Teach us truth, ghosts of antiquity!).

The giant-sized effigies shot into the air one at a time, releasing a divine display of colors, hissing, laughing and moaning as they hovered above the fire pit.

First the Nymph Azel spoke. Attired in a risqué emerald clad tunic, sporting lustrous breasts and a voluptuous body, she exuded the smell of orange blossoms and sweet Baby's Breath.

"I am Azel, presented for your entertainment, brave lovers. Cast chants in my direction, favor me above all other Moods you shall observe tonight. I am a capricious nubile damsel, a charmer of mortal men and gods. I am a siren intent on luring you away from your mission and to shipwreck your soul."

Kubernatos, the Rogue Spirit and brave maritime captain spoke.

"I am the sea captain Kubernatos. Centuries ago, my Trireme vessels and fireboats crashed into the rocky shoreline at Malea during a horrific storm. Seven hundred souls were lost. I am here to pay homage to my deckhands and resolve their drowning sadness."

The Peaceable Spirit, Tranquillitas, entered. A staggering beauty. Purity flowed from her, adorned in a trailing pearl white gown, sinuous brunette hair cascading to her thighs. Her lips were painted with Egyptian red rouge. Her green eyes foretold a history of brutality, yet her poise offset anything offensive, unadulterated in form, harboring no malicious intent.

"I am your Spirit of Peace, Tranquillitas, called here by your forefathers to remove disloyalty from your hearts."

The specter called the Ox appeared. A grayish figure decked out in a sorcerer's hat and sparkling blue robe, holding a divining rod in one hand.

"I am the Ox. Deceiver of many and ultimate antagonist. I devour whom I choose. I seek out any creature claiming entitlement against a suffering comrade and punish him. My ancestry follows from the great generals of ancient times. I am the military genius you have been longing for to vanquish Stella the Diviner and her evil Ruffian hordes."

Lastly, the grand Lovers, Adonis and Minerva came forward. A pastiche of struggling humanity inscribed on each soul. More human than divine. The lovers were taking each other, unashamed, adorned simply in garden vines and leaves.

"I am Adonis. I was gored to death in my preexistence by a vicious boar. I spent half my life above ground and half below the earth before I was resurrected. My eternal devotion is the goddess Minerva. I elected her as my paramour over Aphrodite. My queen gropes me at will, flirting with my manhood and softening me to the point of vulnerability."

"I am Minerva, the goddess of wisdom, art, education and commerce. Adonis is a marvelous paradise, an irreverent creature, full of passion. I am patient and forgiving. He delivers sorrow to me by pleasuring his hoard of concubines, but only after releasing his sperm inside me. He is my Man-God."

"Well, there you have it!" Naomi said pompously. "Enough of this little mythology lesson. Let's get on with the main course. Murtha, bring me the Mender Chalice. It's time we all celebrate this night by passing the hooch around to enrich our dreams."

The chalice was sipped and distributed. When it reached Gretchen and Alice they lunged, almost knocking each other over to get to it. The happy juice was continually refilled by an invisible source to quench their thirsts and make them tipsy.

Jake and Zach finally swaggered in from the oceanfront lugging a huge catch of fish. The girls became electrified with desire upon seeing their returning hunks. In hushed composure, the guys dropped their nets, then subtly guided their lovers toward the starlit beach.

Naomi grinned as she watched the couples walk away. "Gotta love it! I'm so proud of this decadent Mender enclave, and inviting them all here just to satisfy their lustful cravings!"

15

The hypnotic sound of the lapping waves formed the perfect mood for a midnight stroll. The women were still under the Mender spell of transformation, their young, tight bodies swaying provocatively in the moonlight. Jake and Zach were at their sides, acting as tour guides to lead them astray in every way.

"I'll take my beautiful date Gretchen north along the coastline," said Jake.

"Cool, and I'll take Abby southward toward her sensual fate," chimed in Zach.

Jake and Gretchen hiked barefoot in the sand for several miles, finally choosing to wade out onto a large sand bar where they bent down to build a sand castle.

Boss man wallowed in desire. "Baby, the sand is almost as moist as the feeling of your inner thighs when I've taken you over and over again."

"Damn, Jake, this is better than Bois d'Arc Lake where we camped under the stars and made love in the tent. It's so refreshing here, there's no annoying people around to spy on us. We've got all night long to celebrate."

Jake could sense she was sexually frustrated and wanted to make the best of it. He took Gretchen's hands and let her caress his chest. She felt him up and down, then they took turns fondling each other. She unleashed her inner ravenous siren, intent on seducing him in the surf. She grabbed his hair and pulled his chiseled face toward her ripe mouth. She saturated his lips with forbidden kisses and flicked her serpentine tongue while inhaling his breath aromas, then felt his hardness press against her in reply.

Gretchen's adrenaline rush was a newfound power. She flipped Jake like a rag doll onto the sand. He sprawled out on his back, peering at her with charmed and eager eyes. She knew he meant business, but trumped him with her erotic improvisations.

She straddled his rock solid body.

"Shut the fuck up, Jake! I'm in control now." Gretchen commanded. His moaning was the only communication she allowed, covering his mouth with her open palm whenever he tried to say something.

All Jake could do was lay back and enjoy the spectacle.

Jake's beefy, firm tool was at Gretchen's complete mercy. She sucked that meat intensely, watching his package grow into full manhood. She broke two fingernails while pulling her claws down his sides, starting the sadistic maneuver just below Jake's armpits and ending at his muscular upper thighs. He moaned with pleasurable strains and relinquished control, approving of her acts of dominance over his body, mind and soul.

The sensation of lording over him was magnificent. Gretchen stuffed his engorged unit in her warm, wet vagina, while her hips locked on, gliding back and forth in deep syncopated rhythms. Gretchen wanted to experience his warm love-jelly shoot up inside her, but had more work to do to achieve the goal. She twerked his nipples and pulled his golden brown grove of chest hair to make him submit. Jake's eyes rolled back in his head as he neared a stupendous orgasm, but at the last moment he gently rolled her over to switch positions.

They engaged in sizzling, supple embraces. The salty ocean water slapped over them, depositing sand and tingly bubbles on their tanned skin. Jake ground his rock-hard penis into Gretchen's swollen honey pot, rocking to-and-fro in sync with the surf. She impatiently groped his tight ass and petted that flaming hot poker stick into submission. Each fleshly stroke sated her more than the last.

He cupped Gretchen's face with his palms, then cast love bites on her neck and ear while whispering sweet nothings. "You're so beguiling, Gretch. Allow me to release my seed inside you," he begged. "Beginning tonight, my dripping *love cream* is the only thing that'll ever fill you up. Our hearts beat as one, sweetheart."

Gretchen tugged at Jake's ass and made him speed things up until she lost complete control of her beautiful young body.

Bam! Jake arched up and ejaculated. His throbbing dick made Gretchen spin off multiple, deep and gratifying climaxes in unison.

Head rush! Body rush! Mind rush! Spirit rush! Spellbinding release.

Intertwined with the universe. Their eyes twinkling, the giggling and smiles, followed by Gretchen's tears of joy.

To cool off, they swam naked across the harbor, returning to their yacht. Settling into Jake's quarters in a delightful repose, they chugged some spiced rum...afterglow, rapturous snuggles, falling into a deep sleep.

16

"Get a grip and wake the hell up!" Callie insisted. But Gretchen's scintillating journey between the two worlds had taken its toll on her body. All sprawled out in her bed comatose, bereft of Jake again after returning from the Mender harbor, she was a sight for sore eyes.

Callie unleashed her beloved pet Rottweiler Romeo, to perform what dogs do instinctively: lick, slobber, and then lick some more.

The plan succeeded to rouse Gretchen, but it wasn't pretty.

"Goddamn, Romeo's saliva's caked on my face, and why all this sand in my bed and on my skin?"

"Uh, what do you expect, sis? While the house was being pummeled by that quirky storm, you and Abby decided to abandon Romeo and me and go on that dreamlike yacht cruise. Hope it was worth it."

"Yes it was, Callie. Jake and Zach invited you too, but you wanted to stay here, remember? You missed out on one badass adventure!"

"Don't rub it in, Gretch."

"Honestly though, this is the first time I've returned from Jake's all pissed off. It's never supposed to be this way."

"In what way?" Callie asked.

"It wasn't my time to leave him. We were all cuddled up in his big boat's cabin asleep after building sandcastles on the beach. The guests at the bonfire all suggested I could settle down there, but still no joy. This constant jerking back and forth between worlds is making me hyperventilate. To fall asleep next to Jake with his arms wrapped securely around me, and then...poof! The next minute I'm expelled back home to deal with this drama, would make anybody flip out."

"Well, Gretch, sorry to burst your bubble, but you were called home by someone other than Naomi."

Gretchen exploded in panic.

"What the fuck are you saying? Who's the one responsible for taking me away from Jake? I refuse to be a lab rat in some perverse magic show!"

"I'm afraid to put you on the spot, Gretch, but one of your spiritualist friend's is visiting. She's in your den, studying that ghastly picture of Jake in the coffin. Do you mind if I call her to your bedside to explain the situation?"

"Oh my God! Is Miranda here? Why didn't you say something earlier, sis?"

Callie nodded smugly and handed sis a bathrobe. Then she motioned for Romeo to fetch Miranda.

Gretchen's voice waivered as she watched Romeo dash out of the room. "Where'd Romeo learn to do that trick? He's no Retriever."

Callie giggled under her breath.

Minutes later Romeo led Miranda into the bedroom.

"Well, hello dear, let me give you a big hug! Thanks to your sister Callie, I've finally been able to bring you home."

Gretchen was speechless.

"Sorry, Miranda. My sister's not in the best of moods. I'm gonna get her some tomato soup and crackers before she passes out with hunger. You two need the time alone anyways."

Miranda took a chair and scooted over to the bedside.

"Remember the crystal ball monitoring instrument Jake gave you, Gretchen? It's quite a powerful magnetic and thermal imaging device.

It's still sitting on the kitchen table where you left it. Thank goodness your Moldavite tummy piercings are working, because I reached out to you in desperation after all those terrible visions came to visit me the past few nights."

Gretchen quivered in terror.

"Is Abby all right?"

"Yes, she's back home recovering from the trip just like you."

Gretchen sighed in relief.

"Tell me what exactly you're experiencing in your dreams, Miranda. Do they concern Jake and me? Are we gonna be okay?"

"Sweetie, it's much bigger than you two. I've been having visions of profane happenings at Burkburnett graveyard. I entered your past memories during a dream. I remember seeing you walk beside Jake the first night you met him under the moonlight. He warned you, but you didn't notice the creatures attempting to block your access to that cemetery. You were under severe attack, but they didn't touch you."

Gretchen turned white.

"You're fucking kidding me, aren't you, Miranda? This whole thing's becoming too damn creepy for my level of comfort."

"Please, Gretch, just hear me out. I'm acting as your advisor because I want you safe."

"Fine, but I'm exhausted and don't want to have nightmares over this. Can you make it quick?"

"I'll try, girl. So like I was saying, there's shadow entities at work out there. But because you have unusual powers, they can't stop you from crossing through the energy threshold to see Jake, at least not yet."

"What about Harrold and Alice?"

"They've already transformed, you know that, right? Didn't you see them in the next world?"

Gretchen looked sheepish.

"Uh, yeah. I just met them at the Mender bonfire and they seemed completely happy. Why can't I be that way with Jake?"

"Gretch, they were at the final stages of the Hazing ritual when we saw them at Alice's gravesite, remember?"

"Okay, but that night was all blurry. Just please return to the topic of why I'm in such danger."

"Sure. Burkburnett has some sort of undulating spirit-barrier surrounding it. No normal human is capable of breaching it, that's why the plots are so messy and unkempt. The other day reports came in from the local news that two kids were riding bikes out there; they ran home screaming. Unexplained fresh burn marks and bruises appeared around their arms and necks, and their bikes were vandalized. It's my opinion a malevolent entity is feasting on the negativity and anxiety from bereaved souls out there, and is becoming intertwined with that place, spawning a mass of supernatural events."

Gretchen shivered with fright.

Callie almost dropped the hot cup of soup she was carrying. The bad vibes hit her like a brick wall when she entered the bedroom.

"Steady, girls. We'll work through this mess together, and figure out what the source of all the conflict is between Gretchen and Jake from a paranormal standpoint."

Miranda caringly placed a Lepidolite necklace around Gretchen's neck. "This should help calm you down," she reassured. "But I do have a final request before I leave so you two can get some rest."

"What's that?" Callie asked.

"In order to provide proper forensics, allow me to borrow Jake's Mender scroll for a few days to see if it yields any clues, okay?"

"Sure thing, have at it," Gretchen said.

"Thanks, and sweet dreams, girls..."

17

Burkburnett Cemetery was a monster, releasing its gruesome secrets when authorities stumbled upon a red colored substance similar to blood, spattered throughout the surrounding undergrowth. Something mysterious had been dragged around, forming tracks leading to nowhere. DNA and chemistry tests proved indiscernible; no traces of human or animal elements were found on the specimen samples, but it gave off an infrared energy.

Investigators set up a staging area on the property just before sunset, then utilized a type of black light instrument attached to a small drone to scan from a thousand feet up. The flying machine recorded a dull glow emanating from the ground, in the shape of a crescent moon, the precise outline of the cemetery, as though something encircled it to mark its territory.

Miranda was called in by the local sheriff's office to decipher things. Performing a psychic investigation was an irresistible offer; she was hopeful any evidence could also help shed light on Gretchen's and others' misfortunate events out there.

"Officers, I acquired an intriguing ancient manuscript," said Miranda. "But regrettably, I'm unable to divulge the owner, due to client privilege. It sounds like Druid prose, but at closer inspection it takes on extraterrestrial qualities. The words allude to human sacrifices, and cautions about impending cataclysmic spiritual warfare."

"Lay that parchment out on the table and we'll determine whether the content warrants us placing it into evidence," chief detective Tippet said. "Reports of some angry bully harassing passersby are flooding in from concerned parents and children who are being spooked in the vicinity. Miranda, don't you think that red substance painted around the graveyard has to do with something notorious?"

Miranda carefully rolled out Jake's composition on the investigator's table.

"Yeah, the happenings could all be related. See here, this manuscript was stowed away in my girlfriend's dog's chew toy. She told me it was sent to her through some cosmic gateway."

Everyone except Miranda busted out laughing.

"Excuse me? Um, have I missed your inside jokes or what?" she pleaded.

"Ma'am, pardon the outburst," said detective Tippet, "but see what you've brought in? It's nothing more than a weathered old newspaper from Egypt or something. Someone's been playing tic-tac-toe and hangman on the sheet, it's all mere scribble and babble."

Miranda had a tizzy fit, grabbed the letter and fumed out of the precinct.

"So much for trying to get this puzzle solved the traditional way," she muttered in frustration.

She stomped to her car and travelled the long stretch of winding road from Burkburnett back to Saint Germaine.

The journey homeward afforded Miranda the solitude to clear her mind. She turned on a Country Western station and settled in, humming to the lyrics.

It was nearing dusk.

Whoa! The horizon is cast in such pretty pastel colors; I can't tell where the sky ends and earth begins.

Ahead five-hundred yards a farmer's tractor was stirring up a cloud of dirt. A stiff southern breeze carried the thick clay particles toward her car. Miranda accelerated, hoping to outrun the grimy veil, but it engulfed her vehicle.

Visibility was at zero.

Damn I hate the feeling of being tossed around like a feather.

A dynamic energy overtook her car, causing it to shake and rattle. During the disturbance, the radio was affected by interference. Hissing like a snake, it skipped through AM and FM stations as though probing the airwaves, then shut off. A screechy white noise flooded the speakers. To make matters worse, Miranda's cell phone lost its signal.

Whatever the hell's out there's got my full attention.

The engine power was cut off and the automobile took on a mind of its own. Manically she pumped the brake and jerked at the wheel, but the beast wouldn't cooperate.

The jalopy finally coasted to a halt near an underpass miles from where the incident began.

Her psychic intuition led her to an ominous conclusion. *I've gotta outwit this robotic entity before it kills me!*

Miranda frantically swung open the driver's door, thrashing like a tangled insect trying to escape a spider's fangs.

Disoriented, she felt someone in the shadows watching her.

Sheltered under a highway overpass, a petite old woman was sitting in a rocking chair tending to a small campfire.

"Excuse me, ma'am," Miranda yelled. "Um, can you tell me in what direction is Saint Germaine?"

The woman responded silently by shaking her head, then waived for Miranda to approach her makeshift encampment.

The last minutes of sundown provided just enough light for Miranda to cross over the highway ahead of the growing darkness.

"Old woman...how do I...wait, that face! Holy fuck! You're not old at all! *Naomi*?"

As Miranda was about to explode in rage, Naomi pointed to the small kettle she had been stirring.

"My, my, Miranda," she said in a condescending tone, "Anger doesn't quite become an apprentice enchantress like you, does it?"

"Naomi, my gut feeling tells me everything about this scene has some hidden meaning. What in heaven's name are you up to?"

"Don't you recognize this place, dear one? Or have I asked the wrong person? I thought by now your coziness with Gretchen Lanners would yield truth about this spot. Sadly, she stills blames me for Jake's accident which happened here three years ago."

Miranda's eyes took on a wildness and her heart sank.

"So you're not that *Tommie entity* after all, the one that sent images of that sexy woman to Jake's phone three years ago? Gretchen swears it was her fault she lost control and lunged at him with that camping knife after seeing the nasty texts. He rushed out of Bois d'Arc Lake campground in his truck and hauled ass until crashing."

"No, of course not!" Naomi interrupted. "I'm an agent of reconciliation, not the Grim Reaper. Miranda dear, this is a sacred place. Behind me stands the Shoal Creek overpass where Jake met his fate with that tanker rig. The concrete buttress to my left is where the impact and fireball occurred. The charcoal black areas mark the spot where steel, flesh and fuel all mingled. It was Stella who caused Jake and Zach's untimely deaths, with many more innocent souls to follow if we don't stop her."

Miranda was seething with disgust. "I don't know who to believe anymore."

Out of the sky a Gatherer creature soared in from Naomi's realm. Its claws extended and tore out a piece of Miranda's hair, then flapped away into the night sky.

"Okay, stop this bullshit, this is exactly what I'm talking about!" Miranda yelled while grabbing at her scalp. She placed her open palm facing Naomi and recited a chant.

"You are powerless to inflict any spells or curses on me, young woman!" Naomi countered.

At that moment a snow white turtle dove floated down from above, landing on Naomi's shoulder. It cooed in sultry tones as Naomi stroked its silky feathers, coaxing the bird to release Miranda's strands of hair from its beak.

"You're insane crazy old harassing hag! My lawyers are gonna prosecute your ass when I get home!"

Miranda set off for her car.

"No so fast! Look here!" Naomi asserted. "Your hair samples completes Gretchen's Virgin Hazing formula. Don't you want to set Gretchen free to be with Jake, the culmination of her entire existence and her ultimate desire? I sent for you because your powers as her medium are sufficient to deliver this mixture for her ultimate healing. If you follow my instructions, Gretchen's grief sickness will be replaced with spirit ripeness through the Virgin Hazing ritual that *you will be capable to perform in my stead.*"

Naomi reached down into the bowl and pulled out two small objects dripping in the bubbly froth.

"I retrieved this dried blood and pieces of Jake's hair directly where my fleet are planted. Stella missed these articles of Jake's earthy essence. In so doing, I'm placing these remnants into a storage vial and entrusting it with you to bring home. You'll receive additional instructions on how to finalize this Hazing recipe so those two love birds can reach full transformation. Are you up for this, Miranda?"

Miranda solemnly bent down on one knee to receive the ingredients, then kissed Naomi's hands.

"Return to your car, young psychic, and resume your travels homeward. Your transportation is now in working order. We'll be in touch through creative visions very soon."

18

Miranda's alliance with Naomi was a brilliantly conceived affair. Upon returning home, her first order of business was to devise a meeting with Jake, most likely an improbable feat. He was existing in the Mender habitat, light years away from earth.

Jake had been showing his human side lately, unpleasant behavior for a Man-God like Jake. All his buddies, including Zach, Harrold, Alice, Rinaldo and the Countess Isabella, were concerned about his growing despondency over Gretchen. The Ruffian blockade at Burkburnett had thwarted his entrance back into her world, making him go stir crazy.

Jake sought some solitude to clear his mind. One evening at the Mender habitat, he was strolling on the same strand of beach where earlier, Gretchen and he had built a sand castle and made exquisite love.

Jake mumbled under his breath the fears and blessings of their love affair, "I'm so out of sorts up here. The human part of me won't stop yearning for her, it's ridiculous. Man, when we dated I thought I'd reach heaven's gateway. It was Gretchen's nature to grant me progress, then she'd stall out and cancel her affections for no logical reason.

She always said she wanted her freedom, but from what? Freedom from true love? I stuck with her when she would inject toxic things into her veins, or get in trouble with the law.

She came running back to me when she wanted a strong shoulder to lean on. Thinking she needed me, I'd develop a false sense of security. Then she'd randomly allow other men to salivate and snatch up her sweetness instead!

Now I'm here in this idyllic Garden of Eden without my soul mate. Part of me wants to believe she really loves me. Is it vanity to fix things right so she feels at home next to me? I mean, she's already taken tons of risks coming up here. And that new sexy body of hers matches my manhood perfectly! I was older than her back on earth, but that doesn't matter anymore?

Hopefully she feels secure enough to venture out and let Naomi perform the Virgin Blood Hazing. We deserve to walk this beach, laugh into the wind and celebrate a lifetime together without fear of pain or suffering. She has my heart over a barrel, and she knows it. And deep down she knows the baby she lost was ours.

Maybe I'm the only soul on earth who understands her bipolar episodes, where her thoughts are scattered to the four corners of the earth. Her brain smolders with heated embers, willing to ignite at a moment's notice because she's enraptured in her fickleness. I want to believe her spirit is tethered to mine.

I'm her grounding, the pole where she can mount and display her capriciousness. I'm unmovable in my love for her, but she remains indifferent to my romantic intentions unless it suits her needs. Then she's like a pouncing lion, ambushing my soul, entertaining fleeting passions and leaving me to languish while my blood spills forth to attract the scavengers. Yet I persist, because I adamantly refuse to relinquish the trophy of my desires unless death do us part.

I saw fire in her eyes that night at Bois d'Arc Lake, when the Harvest Moon was at its zenith…maybe she was justified brandishing that hunting knife and cutting me open. I peeled out of the campground upset and then suddenly died on her at Shoal Creek overpass. Perhaps I should've handled it all better…"

Jake's lamentation over Gretchen was so severe, his melancholy surged like a tidal wave and inundated the Mender hyperspace frequencies.

Gretchen was busy at the salon getting her hair colored, when his vibes rocketed toward earth and flooded her spirit. Overwhelmed, she turned to Miranda for counsel.

They came together at True Bloods, their old stomping grounds. By the time Miranda arrived, Gretchen was lit with booze.

"Damn, girl, you're clutching that beer mug so tightly your knuckles are all white," Miranda poked.

"I'm just trying to understand why all of a sudden Jake's powerless to come see me. It's like he's locked away in solitary confinement and all I get are his faint sounds of anguish."

"Consider me as your intercessor. Both of you have different methods to cope with the pain, I understand that. But just don't misconstrue Jake's non-verbal feelings as anything more than a form of love expressiveness."

"I'm confused, Miranda. He's already transformed and is finally showing signs of missing me. Isn't his nature supposed to be nearing perfection? Naomi calls it 'spirit ripeness.'"

"Jake isn't as superhuman as you think, Gretch."

The comment irritated her.

"Stop being so smug, Miranda. You've never spent time alone with my man like I have. And your wizardry is far from perfect. At last check, I can change into a hot, young babe with the insatiable appetite for fucking the shit outta Jake, not you."

"I'll overlook your tipsiness, cause I realize you'll stop at nothing to preserve your youthful look, Gretch. But it's only bestowed on you when you travel through the Mender passageways. Every time you return home, you lose it."

"Yeah, it sucks. Thanks for reminding me of the obvious!"

"Hun, I'm sorry, but unless we can figure out a way to break through the Ruffian blockade at Burkburnett, there won't be any more sexy transformations."

"What about my closet? It's a gateway to Jake's place!"

"Nah, Naomi said the only access now is through the main portal, which is located at Burkburnett. Stella's crew threw up one hell of an impenetrable wall. Its negative energies are so awful, it's seeped into the human realm. You saw the news about all those children being attacked by the Ruffian shadow entities. It's so hostile out there, you may never see Jake again unless you follow Naomi's suggestions with blind faith."

Gretchen paused and reflected on her words.

"If you're asking me to trust you, then I'm all ears, Miranda."

"Okay. Well, Naomi's already issued me several telepathic messages, critical intel disclosing the precise spot where the main portal to Jake's world is located."

"Where's that?" Bug-eyed Gretchen asked.

"Access is only granted at the base of the old Bois d'Arc tree during a full moon, but since the entire place is surrounded by her sentries, only the Virgin Hazing will give you penetrable inner strength to purge the place of that filthy Ruffian infection."

Gretchen sneered. "Then what the fuck are we waiting for?"

"It's pretty complicated and real risky. Don't forget, we're dealing with vindictive creatures whose primary goal is to disrupt lovers from reuniting," stated Miranda. "Even Jake's scroll referred to the Hazing as 'Not for the faint of heart.' I have the basic formula for starting the process, but it's far from a slam dunk."

"Is it a potion? I'm already familiar with the chalice drinks. Those refreshers make me so giddy and horny around Jake. I'm sure Abby's missing Zach real bad too."

Miranda shook her head, then glanced down.

"What's wrong?" Gretchen asked. "Is it Abby? Is she mad at me?" She hasn't responded to any of my texts lately. Hell, hang tight and I'll just call her..."

"Gretch, put down your phone. Naomi's granted me the ability to receive visions now, but what I experienced last night is troubling and downright depressing."

Gretchen almost lunged at Miranda. "What the fuck are you saying? Just shoot straight with me! Where's my friend?"

"Alright, I'm afraid Abby's a lost cause. In my dream yesterday, I watched Stella trick her into visiting a place called Lover's Purgatory. Now she's in bondage and will never see Zach again."

"Goddamnit! Stella needs to back the fuck down. Where is this Lover's Purgatory that you mention? I'll hire me some badass vigilantes and rescue her myself."

"Uh, it would be a miracle if we ever locate her again. Lover's Purgatory exists in this sphere, but there's no specific street address. It could be any nursing home, mental hospital where people are bed ridden or in wheelchairs, and heavily sedated. Instead of taking on the form of a sexy siren, poor Abby most likely was camouflaged to appear like a rehab patient recovering from a bad accident, and was undoubtedly hypnotized to forget her own name and identity. She's destined to grieve so intensely for Zach, she'll go insane and die a lonely soul, separated from her true love for eternity. Neither of them will be fulfilled. Only Stella can inflict such acts of torture on true lovers."

"Then unleash the Mender formula!" Gretchen shouted. "I'll do whatever it takes to fulfill my destiny! Stand back world, you don't know what's coming!"

19

News arose from the Mender habitat that Stella's Ruffian force had posed as imposters, invading and ransacking the Mender storehouses. The Tools of Transformation—the Chalices, partially weaved Mender scarf materials, and a large quantity of crystals and magic stones were wiped out. The loss of match-maker inventory marked a period of declining soul mate attraction, lack of spirit ripeness and the shutdown of portal travels throughout the sphere.

Anyone allied with Naomi and outfitted with the Mender Tools were targeted. The graveyard was one such ambush zone, a seething cesspool of Ruffian malevolent behavior.

Naomi's airborne creatures—the Chalice Doves, Menders and Gatherers, were getting the brunt of Stella's pissyness. She was insanely jealous of their matchmaking abilities. Supernatural nets and traps were being rigged by the Ruffian gangsters to catch them while in progress of seizing hair samples or delivering love potions to newly reunited couples.

To keep her elixir vats safe, Naomi and her core group of creatures traversed the uppermost mountaintop of the Mender biosphere, where they stashed the supplies of youthful drink. She reestablished communique with her earthen entities by using celestial cloud formations as frequency hopping points to avoid being intercepted, hacked or deciphered.

Sex gods such as Jake and Zach, as well as any fully transformed couples weren't at risk, since their auras had reached full Mender maturity, too strong to penetrate. Instead, she set her sights on the low-hanging fruit like Abby, those vulnerable, lonely souls who constantly begged to cross over to meet up with their lost lovers at any cost.

Stella's brothel infiltrated Burkburnett, inflicting further chaos on the graveyard. She preselected certain visitors and allowed them access through her Ruffian blockades if they radiated high levels of grief pheromones. She positioned her Nymphets near the crypts holding candelabras in one hand, and fake images of the deceased laid out in coffins in the other hand. As the cemetery guests made their way through the labyrinth of headstones to their lovers' plots, they observed risqué dancers performing striptease acts in the shadows, chanting voodoo and mocking the dearly departed. The Ruffians shapeshifted to appear like other despondent visitors. They functioned as emotional bait to lure heartbroken humans toward a trap door located directly behind the headstones. It was the gateway to Lover's Purgatory, the passageway where earlier Abby had succumbed and disappeared.

The idea of rescuing enslaved souls brought out the best in Gretchen. She became a crusader in search of Abby, but still relied on the psychic powers of Miranda to guide her into the abyss of Lover's Purgatory. Together they crafted a stealthy game plan to enter the cemetery undetected, cloaked by the powers of the Mender scarfs.

Miranda and Gretchen arrived at Burkburnett around midnight. The local authorities had set up a crime scene station, with yellow 'Do not cross' tape hung on the gargoyle gate entry point to warn potential trespassers.

"Craziest thing I've ever seen," barked chief Tippet, as he met the girls ambling up the trail toward his investigation unit. "There's no damn evidence except that unidentifiable red substance swabbed all over the brush, and complaints from parents that their children are being taunted. I don't want bad publicity or some national news channel picking up this story, but if we can't figure out how to short out the invisible energy field and regain access to the property, the FBI will take over and my hands will be tied."

"With all due respect, sir, I've brought my associate Gretchen here, to assist me. I think we can crack the nut wide open, but need a private area to rehearse our plan."

Officer Tippet chuckled. "Second time's a charm, lady? Did you bring your little Ouija board and bag of spells to fight off the goblins?"

"When you mock the dead, you also mock the living, Mr. Tippet," Gretchen glumly warned.

Tippet got all ruffled by her comment. He shook his head as though beaten by the insults game, then motioned for the girls to use the mobile forensic trailer as their private meeting place.

Once inside, they sorted out their strategy to breach Naomi's underground lair

"What we're about to undertake is a rescue ops mission, Gretch. The only way we can penetrate Stella's wall of defense is to invoke geokinetic invisibility."

Gretchen was bemused.

"Not trying to stump you, girl. I'll translate the metaphysical lingo. It simply means *we'll utilize a Moldavite stone from my stash, combined with your Mender scarf to become invisible.* We have to work fast, as the spell will break at sunrise, which is only three hours from now."

The mood was solemn as Miranda brought forth a fist-sized Moldavite crystal and instructed Gretchen to wrap the Mender scarf around it to make a sling-like object.

They huddled together. Gretchen whirled the sling around their heads until they felt a strong magnetic sensation pass through their bodies, making them light headed. She recited a chant which Miranda repeated before passing out, 'Powerful Menders, change us into transparent beings, undetectable to Stella and her hoard; lead us to Abby's tortured soul and unleash her suppressed desires to reunite with Zach, for he's waiting on the other side.'

In the twinkling of an eye, the girls nonchalantly strolled up to the police checkpoint where a few of the officers were standing. Miranda stared down one of the men squarely in the face to test her new nature, but he didn't flinch.

"Watch this!" Miranda whispered.

She inched up and blew a strong kiss at the officer. He drew back and slapped at his cheek, as though trying to squash a mosquito, disturbed by the unseen annoyance.

They broke into chuckles. "Well, one thing for sure, Gretch, no other humans can see us, but at least we can see each other."

"Here, Gretch, hold on to one of these, they act as lamplights to navigate us safely through Stella's pit of darkness."

Miranda handed her a large Lepidolite crystal. They proceeded like two secret agents past the police barrier, creeping ever so near the gravesites.

20

Gretchen's Mender chant ushered them into a sixth dimension reality. Entering the new continuum made them feel high as kites, floating, not walking; reacting with supple, translucent bodies and possessing 360 degree night vision.

They crossed near *plot number one*, where a pair of Ruffian bouncers stood at attention. Their extremities resembled a wasp's, with folded wings and spikey body hair spread all around their torsos. Protruding feelers were visible above their helmets, curling slightly to pick up the scents and vibrations from the night air.

The girls operated in stealth mode, shuffling past the Ruffians unnoticed, with only their instincts to guide them.

"Hey, girl," Miranda whispered. "Do you feel the cold and warm pockets of air stream by?"

"Yeah, I was gonna ask you the same thing," said Gretchen. "It's a really weird sensation."

"Well, avoid the chilly pouches, they're the spirits of lost love who're condemned to loneliness. They float around here in perpetual sadness, even on sweltering summer nights their chill never dissipates. We need to tuck ourselves under the warmer currents; they're forms of vitality flowing from the frog pond where life exists peaceably. Tap into it and extract the organic energy source, it'll enhance our performance like steroid injections. Stella can throw up random force fields at a moment's notice to block our progress. She's a sneaky one, so we need all the help we can get!"

They made their way through the sea of grave markers, from the periphery where the fresher sod was laid, until they reached the center of the graveyard. Weather-beaten and fractured headstones constructed in the early eighteenth century populated the rows.

"This is some jaunt through time, Miranda."

"More like we're being sent into the wilderness, hot on the trail of a henchman who takes pleasure in desecrating sacred burial sites," Miranda quipped.

Burkburnett began to reveal its forbidden secrets.

"Wow, Miranda! Check out all the red rose pedals that've been strewn about."

"I see a glob of 'em. It's almost like someone's purposely planted them to lead us to a specific destination."

Miranda picked up a specimen.

"Interesting. The buds aren't completely dried yet. The discoloration and wilt marks indicate they're only a few hours old. In Druid lore, these represent the pathway of a suffering soul relinquishing suppressed desires. This time of year all the rose bushes are dormant around here. Whoever was carrying these knew what they were doing."

"Kinda like an S.O.S signal?" Gretchen thought.

"Yep."

The girls followed the rose pedal trail several yards, until they approached a mausoleum-type tomb located at the far end of the cemetery. The white gothic marble appeared fresh and in perfect condition.

"Gretch, notice the tall obelisk headstone is void of any name, suggesting either the person's still alive, or died a shameful death."

"Yeah, this place gives me the creeps. Observe the moonlight? It's hitting every grave except this one, almost like there's some black shadow draped over the crypt deflecting the moonbeams."

"Well, my bladder's aching for relief with all this excitement," Miranda said. "Thank goodness we're invisible to those Ruffians, cause I might just unload my torrent of piss right here if I don't find an outlet pretty soon."

They broke into hysterical laughter.

The sound of a creaky door hinge jolted the girls from their light hearted mood. It was followed by a blast of freezing subterranean air which jutted from the abyss, releasing a plume of steam as it hit the tepid night air. In so doing, the event revealed the way into Stella's burrow. She'd cleverly masked the entrance to Lover's Purgatory with a patch of knee-high weeds, but now a naked feminine form with jet black dreadlocks emerged, boasting a tattoo of a slithering rattlesnake and skull head. The reptilian image extended from her lower stomach to the middle of her nipple-ring breasts.

"I am Stella the Diviner, join my virgin brothel, and I'll change you into a sexy Playboy Bunny, where you'll get all the dick you want!"

Gretchen twitched nervously and shoved her elbow into Miranda's side. She doubled over in pain.

"Sorry, Miranda, but I wanted you to take notice of the cruel bitch popping out of that hole. You'd recognize that silhouette anywhere. She's gloating over her female pimp status, that goddamn self-promotor, trying to recruit innocent girls like me into her brothel by promising tummy tucks, fake boobs and a full time rockin' hard body! Stella's already amassed a rag tag army of naughty, conniving castaways, but I'm not gonna be one of 'em," Gretchen insisted.

"I'm with ya," Miranda reassured, as she massaged her sore rib cage. "Your jab sure did take the wind out of me, but at least Stella can't see or hear us fumble around. I'm kinda enjoying this covert espionage. Let's just sit back and wait for that psychopath to cough up the truth. Maybe our patience will pay off and she'll lead us to Abby."

Stella the Diviner behaved like a tyrant on her throne, issuing decrees to her Ruffian troops by screaming profanities at them. Her ladies-in-waiting, including the erotic dancers and exhibitionists she had dispersed throughout the graveyard, were instructed to congregate at the entrance to her cavern. Stella lit up a cigarette and paced nervously, rehearsing a motivational speech to ensure her hoards were compliant.

"I wish she'd leave this place in its natural state of decay," Gretchen murmured. "That meddlesome cunt's pushing her luck around here."

"Hey, now's our chance, Stella's looking distracted!" Miranda yelped. "She's walking away and leaving that trap door undefended, you ready to pillage her little wasp's nest?"

"Hell yeah! In my wildest dreams I'd never guess I'd rise to become such a tomb raider! Her bad karma's spilling over into innocent lives. She needs to pay."

21

While Stella was dallying in a nearby section of the graveyard, Miranda and Gretchen accessed her secret entry point and took a spiral staircase down to the first level of Lover's Purgatory. It was a grand portico with several spider-webbed tunnels spread out in opposite directions.

"I'm getting a headache just choosing which path to take; I'm certain one of these damn catacombs will lead us to Abby, so our effort's not totally in vain if we screw up and have to back track," Gretchen fumed.

They picked the third tunnel from the right, where muffled, whimpering voices and rattling chains broadcast from somewhere deep within its icy passages.

The spell of invisibility cast upon their bodies was fading, so they had to act fast and locate Abby before being detected. Their feather-light footsteps were barely sufficient to tackle the slippery frosty substance glued to the cavern walls and footpath.

Passing through the tunnel, they descended to another layer of Lover's Purgatory, entering a vast antechamber. The place was packed full of stolen Mender stuff, including numerous precious stones and crystals, half-woven scarfs and chalice cups.

"That fucking thief!" Gretchen yelled. "Naomi will be very interested in retrieving this Mender treasure-trove."

"For sure," agreed Miranda. "I've recorded these precise coordinates for Naomi. We're almost two thousand feet below ground now."

They followed the trail of hauntingly sorrowful sounds, until reaching a subterranean, garish boudoir. Its décor was in the style of a medieval dungeon, with an enormous bed as the centerpiece. Several human figures were chained up to the massive bedposts, which reached the ceiling. Steel cages held prisoners whose shriveled bodies begged for food and water.

Gretchen desperately panned around the room in search of Abby, while Miranda stroked the Lepidolite crystal hanging on her neck to keep them safe from the tormentor.

Several hideous ghouls were attending to the oppressed by squeezing droplets of water from dirty rags onto their tongues.

Miranda objected. "This clammy place reeks of torture! Those persons don't deserve to be treated as subhuman."

A troll holding a rawhide whip was hovering over the bed. A pair of gangly, moaning humanoids with ankle chains and handcuffs appeared from underneath the bed sheets. The disgusting ghouls forced them to take each other. Their heartache was so great, they were shaking, spilling tears and crying out in terror. "Save us, anybody!"

"Stop harming these poor souls!" Gretchen barked.

"They can't see or hear us, remember girl?"

Miranda's eyes lit up as though receiving an epiphany.

"Holy fuck, I'm envisioning what this bordello is used for! Stella's forcing these captives to perform non-consensual sex with each other! It's an abomination against soul mate love. She's sucking whatever hope remains from these hostages and making them zombies. Lover's Purgatory is seething with *counterfeit love!* Stella's obvious intent is to colonize Burkburnett with these tortured souls who're brainwashed into her service. Eventually they'll overrun this place and cut off the inflow of spirt ripe couples to the Mender habitat. Naomi's world is at risk of becoming extinct!"

A young, feminine form staggered in from the shadows. She had a serene face but a scrawny body.

Miranda and Gretchen were bewildered. Their jaws dropped when they realized the effigy was Abby. Miranda pulled out the vial which Naomi had given her at Shoal Creek overpass.

"What exactly are you planning?" inquired Gretchen.

"I'm following Naomi's guidelines, it calls for a dash of tormented tears to complete the Virgin Hazing recipe."

Miranda shuffled to get closer to Abby, but a ghoul appeared acting as her slave master. The despicable creature brought out a chain leash attached to a spiked neck yoke. The steely mechanism made a clicking sound as it locked around Abby's swan throat.

Gretchen reached out in her invisible form to grab Abby's arm, but she passed right through it. The ghoul master reeled in Abby and dragged her across the icy dirty floor toward a large iron cage.

"I can't take seeing her suffer much longer, Miranda." Abby welled up in tears and was losing composure fast.

"Chill out girl, let's not forget our mission. We're here to free Abby and syphon some essential fluids from her tear ducts before we retreat. We need to restore her dignity from this brutality. Notice Abby has no hair? Her form is nothing but a cellophane spiritual substance. Her body lacks flesh and has been somehow detached, most likely deposited by the Ruffians above ground in Saint Germaine."

Thick cloud formations hovered over Burkburnett and masked the moonlight.

"Oh shit, you feeling that eerie sensation, Miranda?"

"Yeah, I think our invisibility gig is up; damn, we're being expelled from the sixth dimension and reentering the cruddy old earthly existence."

Their toes tingled from the shooting pain of the broken spell. The sensation of being dunked into a bucket of hot water saturated their bodies and made its way up to their heads. The shock of being converted back to human flesh and bone jarred them while Stella's minions looked on with baited breath.

"Fuck it, they see us now! I only have a nanosecond to get my tear sample from Abby before we get busted!"

By now Abby was already in confinement, slumped over on the frozen dungeon floor, nearly overdosed with tranquilizers. Pieces of a barren, thorny red rose stem were scattered throughout the cell. Miranda flung her arms between the cage bars, extending the open vial near Abby's face. She snatched Abby's silken tears in midair, then rushed away with Gretchen in tow, glancing back once to pay one final respect to Abby's spirit body.

22

The girls operated like escape artists, fleeing ahead of the Ruffian watchmen into the dim tunnels of Lover's Purgatory. Miranda clutched the flask of love potion to protect it at all cost, but their luck finally ran out. At the end of one section of grotto appeared a diviner's fire which discharged volleys of electrical current into the lining of the tunnel. The girls were under attack by the mysterious force of energy, as though being slow roasted on a skewer. Within the fiery mass, a sinister voice rang out.

"Hey you two little skanks, who the fuck do you think you are trying to disrupt my enterprise down here?" Stella the Diviner scolded.

In a desperate move to shun her, the girls closed their eyes and turned to bear hug one another. "I just want to wake up from this sordid nightmare, tell me when it's all over," pleaded Gretchen.

A seismic event similar to an earthquake crashed down from above. The rocky buttresses shook and the pathway heaved to and fro like thrashing waves, stunning everyone, including Stella, who cast a deer-in-the-headlights look at the girls.

Stella was surveying the mayhem, when the dark outline of an animal with bared fangs and a red bandana bolted out of nowhere and rattled off forceful growls and barks. "Good boy, Romeo, yes, that's our enemy!" a voice from behind the girls decreed.

The ladies spun around and saw two gallant knights mounted bareback on white Arabian stallions wielding Roman Gladius swords. Abby's spirit body was draped over one of the men's horse saddle.

"Oh my God! Here comes my honey!" Gretchen shouted triumphantly. "I knew Jake and Zach would save us!"

"Jump on my horse, we've plotted the escape route to your freedom!" Jake announced.

Abby's spirit body came alive and her mind awakened during the chaos. Everyone was overjoyed to witness her sudden recovery.

"Babe, my fate was sealed the moment I came to visit your grave site last night looking for you."

"What are you talking about, darling?" Zach asked.

"Stella lured me to Burkburnett, along with several other visitors when the Harvest Moon was at its peak. She propped up an impenetrable force field to keep everyone out. You and Jake couldn't reach out to me, cause she simultaneously blocked the Mender frequencies between our worlds, but I got lucky and she let me in. I was strolling through the cemetery and one of her exotic dancers flashed a picture of you lying dead in your coffin with red lipstick smeared on your face, which freaked me out. I had brought some red roses to leave on your headstone so you could sense my presence. I was so vulnerable, I made a covenant with her. Now I'm in a depleted condition, hairless and lack the features you crave in me. I regret selling my soul to Stella, but she made me the deal of a lifetime, promising to make my youthful beauty everlasting. She said I could have access to the Mender habitat without a chaperone and to bypass the Mender portal, since it's so inconvenient. She said I could show up any time, resume having rough sex with you, the type we like, and then seduce you into marrying me. There's just one glitch..."

"Shut the hell up, you babbling slut, you belong to me now!" Stella interjected. "And as far as your loser friends are concerned, none of

you'll ever see the light of day again, so get off your horse meat and submit to me. I'm so goddamn proud to trap my first-ever Mender Man-
Gods! You two are exceedingly stupid to think these little whores have a
future. They're just cheap bait."

Jake and Zach were brave and daring gents who'd trained part time
as combat officers in the Menders Royal Armed Forces (MRAF). They
courageously charged her on their white stallions with bayonets drawn.

The outcome was bleak, for Stella possessed powers exceeding their
combined strengths.

A massive cantilever gearbox and beams rose up from the ground,
blocking access to the escape route.

The horses turned skittish and almost bucked the men off.

Stella reveled with vengeful eyes.

"You hapless punks have nowhere to go; my warriors can outduel
anybody in Naomi's lame kingdom. Abby, I command you to return to
your monkey cage!"

Her Ruffians and dungeon ghouls streamed in for all sides, bent
on subduing and capturing them all. Stella threw a supernatural net
around the group. "This mesh will suck out all your Mender powers and
leave you hapless and helpless."

Brazenly, Zach quickly tied a Mender scarf soaked in Abby's tears
around his sword and raised it high, slicing through a bit of netting,
then issued a Mender chant, "For the sake of true love and honor, I
hereby summon the ancient Mender spirits to save us from these ghetto
gangsters!"

A thunderous boom caused a fissure to form in the apex of the
tunnel, exposing the thriving Bois d'Arc tree clustered in the soil
above them. The tree had a mind of its own, extending and lower-
ing its roots like octopus tentacles to form a ramp connecting them
to safe land.

To ease the burden of their exodus, Jake slung Gretchen on his
horse and galloped up the slope, while Miranda followed. But Stella
wouldn't relent. She shot arrows filled with a neuro sedative at the

escapees. One hit Zach's horse squarely on the rump, which para-lyzed it. The beast snorted wildly, then slumped down in confusion and went numb.

Jake, Miranda and Gretchen reached the summit but refused to leave Zach and Abby's sight.

Several Ruffians stormed over to the befallen victims and placed Abby and Zach in shackles.

Stella gloated over their recapture. "I can't help laughing my ass off at this pathetic scene! Even if your rescue efforts had worked, you'd have to go retrieve her earthen body and reconnect her two parts. I've concealed her *other half* in a very inconspicuous place, so you'd be hard pressed to restore her full essence and vibrancy. In her current state she's worthless. Even Naomi that cuntress would consider Abby a useless wretch."

"Then what do you plan to do with me?" Abby's spirit yelped. "I'm growing lonelier by the hour down here. I refuse to be your sex slave, so just finish me if it suits you."

"Missy, I've got a bigger prize to pursue than you."

Stella pointed her spindly finger up in the direction of Gretchen and rolled off a sarcastic giggle.

"What? You mean Gretchen?" Jake hollered.

"Precisely. Her DNA is such luscious chemistry, after some brain-washing, she'll have the knack to dethrone Naomi someday. Her type will keep my empire running smooth for eons. I want to breed and clone Gretchen."

"You proposing to make us a deal?" Gretchen yelled down.

"No sweetheart! Don't negotiate with that Trollop!" Jake begged.

Stella was throttled by her offer, but persisted. "Um, enlighten me some more, little lady."

"Well, how about me for Abby and Zach? A two-for-one deal. If I'm such a priceless resource, then let them go and I'll come back down the hole right now and subject myself to your whims if you set them loose."

Jake almost went berserk upon hearing Gretchen's offer to switch spots to save Zach and Abby. But Miranda just sat back and nodded her head as though granting her support in a telepathic sort of way.

"Baby, do you know what you're doing?" Jake whispered to Gretchen in angst. "The act you propose will reduce our love affair to a mere memory."

"Jake hun, I've loved you before time began. It's meant to be that Abby and Zach get set free, and I'm happy to take their spots. You just have to find a way to come back and rescue me. I'll be your *damsel in distress*, but promise me you'll rehabilitate Abby the second you leave here. Then unleash hell on this place and eliminate these fuckin' clowns for good."

A Ruffian soldier freed Zach from his chains, then roused Abby's spirit body, motioning for Gretchen to be swapped with her. At first, Jake wouldn't allow Gretchen to leave his presence. The couple locked lips and attempted to calm each other. The little romantic interlude annoyed the living hell out of Stella. "Goddamn, enough already!" she squawked.

"Hey, Stella, back down for just a minute, I've gotta say goodbyes to my prince, Jake Conroe," Gretchen lashed back.

She bravely strode to the cell to supplant Abby's frail essence and held out her arms in submission. Abruptly the guards slapped chains around her wrists, neck and legs.

Jake was close to losing it. "I'll be back for you, dear. You can count on it," he proclaimed in a somber tone, but his chivalrous blood boiled in revenge as he turned to face his small band of allies.

"Guys, we're making a bullseye for the Mender portal which exists in that tree!" he shouted. "It's the central corridor on earth which connects the two spheres together!"

Zach loaded Abby's spirit body onto his stallion and the group dashed up the ramp, hurling themselves directly at the swollen trunk of the Bois d'Arc tree. "Hold on to your ten-gallon hats, Saint Germaine, here we come!"

From nowhere a creature passed by, in the direction of where they had just been, Lover's Purgatory. A loud shriek arose from Stella, "You fuckin' flying goblin, return that chunk of hair to me!"

Jake and Zach looked befuddled and shrugged it off, but Abby in her depressed condition recognized the entity, "Ah, Murtha the Mender? Nicely done, Naomi," she whispered under her breath.

The ground shuddered behind them, like a monster's jowl's coming to life, its energies flicking tons of dirt to backfill Stella's fleapit. Wild flowers and hedges replaced what had remained of the spot, a memorial to Gretchen's captivity.

23

*J*ake's posse entered the Mender portal and hightailed it to Saint Germaine at lightning speed.

They plopped out of the vortex near the back alley of True Bloods saloon.

Jake and Zach peered down to the ground for a split second and uttered some chant while snapping their fingers three times in unison.

Miranda was ruffled. "Fellas, what kind of juju are you stirring up now? Time travel may be slicker than snot, but it makes my hair have split ends. I'm already missing Gretchen, but this place brings back memories, it's where we'd hang out, pop a few cold ones and discuss metaphysical issues."

Everyone dismounted. The white stallions vanished into thin air. Miranda tended to Abby, making sure she was feeling well enough to continue with the escapades.

The sound of burning tires and screeching engine disrupted the placidness of the moment. A speeding SUV with blinding high beams was coming at them, intent on making impact. The driver pounded the brakes just in time, skidding to a halt a few feet from the bystanders.

Romeo sounded off several friendly barks, as though recognizing someone.

The driver bailed out of the vehicle casting a pensive look.

"Sorry guys, I'm a little late, but the main highway was blocked off due to a fatality accident. Thanks for the text message, Jake. How's my sweet sister doin'?"

Miranda yelped. "Callie? Oh my goodness!"

She rushed over to console the weeping Callie. Romeo tried to jump up on Callie and lick her cheek, but Miranda pushed him away.

Jake and Zach let the girls' sentimental feelings percolate for a bit.

"I personally know how painful it is for our loss, Callie, but Gretchen is one damn strong chic. If she were here right now, she'd probably want us to put our feelings aside and get Abby back on track. So let me ask you, Callie, did you bring the Mender surveillance system I sent to you in Romeo's chew toy from a few weeks back?"

Callie wiped away the tears and sniffled.

"Yeah, did I ever! I used that newfangled device to track Gretchen when she went to see you. I could've abused its powers to watch you two... um, well you know...I'm not a voyeur so I spared you the embarrassment of seeing yourselves all..."

Jake and Zach snickered. "Yah, yah, thanks for not finishing the sentence, Callie. Let's cross our fingers and put it to the test again, this time for a higher good," Jake countered.

Callie ran to the car trunk and produced an oval, rocky object.

"Good job, now let's power it up here on your engine hood and take a look," Jake said proudly.

The enchanting Brazilian amethyst geode was a sight for sore eyes. It housed the apparatus and had hinges installed on one side. Once unclasped, the two sides opened into a perfectly symmetrical laptop-looking unit.

"See, amazing Mender technology, don't ya think?" Jake boasted. "The antennae are built-in to the optical transmitter. The signals utilize a modulation and amplitude scheme that is tolerant against atmospheric radiation, gamma rays or even Ruffian interference. It's better than any nanotechnology this planet has to offer."

Jake passed his hand over the stone facade. The circuitry responded with extravagant colors emitted from its crystalline display, initiating a highly sophisticated algorithm to process the whereabouts of Abby's physical body.

"Let's cross our fingers and hope this thing works like a charm. As long as Stella didn't remove Abby's Moldavite tummy ring, we'll get a reading pretty soon.."

"You guys had better hurry and find her!" Miranda yelled. "Things don't look good over here! Abby's effigy is fading fast. There's a symbiotic dependency between her two manifestations, similar to Siamese twins, which require reunification within a certain time frame. She's gonna expire soon."

The machine scanned through thousands of addresses in Saint Germaine.

Several loud beeps and sustained electrifying hums generated from the component.

"Holy smokes! I think we found Abby's other half!" Zach shouted euphorically. Everyone huddled around the car to verify the miracle.

They piled into Callie's car. By this time Abby's spirit body was withering away and gravely ill. Her breaths were irregular and her translucent skin was pallor.

Callie drove at a manic pace, guided by the GPS instruction to the south side of town. The built-in Mender compass locked on to a strong signal positioned behind a nursing home.

"You stay here, Miranda, while Jake and I go for a quick jaunt. If we don't return, please call the police."

"Alright, Zach."

The men ambled through a stretch of sidewalk leading to a dumpster near the back entrance of Gilroy's Manor. A strong stench almost knocked them over. "This garbage reeks, dude," Zach said.

In the shadows laying on its side was a female figure. She was wearing a hospital gown and a medical ID bracelet with the name *Unknown No.5– Mental Ward East* - handwritten in red ink on the band.

Zach could barely contain his emotions, even for a Man-God.

He bent down on one knee and pulled out a single, beautiful red rose from somewhere unknown and placed it under the stray patient's nose.

"Smell the Mender love nectar in this rose, it's for you, babe."

The woman started to heave and cough, as though waking up from a catatonic state.

When her eyesight was steady enough, she looked right at Zach's face and into his big brown eyes, then broke a huge smile.

Zach tested her memory. "Darling, do you know who I am?"

"You're my...uh, my Zach?"

"Yesss I *am* your Zach, and you're my Abby! Now let's get you back to the car pronto, so synthesis with your disembodied spirit can occur before your ageless qualities fade away forever!"

The reunification between Abby's celestial form and terrestrial body was an event to behold. In the car they were placed side by side, as Jake brought forth a Mender chalice filled with sustaining and nourishing fluids. The solution bonded the two entities into one, starting with the hair and head, and progressed to the limbs and chest.

Head as one, hair as one, heart as one, eyesight as one, touch as one.

News of Zach's daring rescue of Abby and her bodily rejuvenation spread throughout the Mender kingdom.

24

Stella had miscalculated the talents of Naomi's fearless and brilliant Men-God in their quest for true love's reconciliation.

Out of spite, she inflicted Gretchen with more sadness – coercing her to cough up secrets regarding the Mender love elixir and Naomi's whereabouts.

Jake fumed with anger and prepared to retaliate.

As foretold in the Mender scrolls, the season was ripe for the 'Virgin Hazing, to save a Mender princess from her plight.' Jake knew what he had to perform in order to free Gretchen from her chains and mend their love affair.

Naomi had entrusted Miranda with the Mender flask to initiate the Hazing ritual. Samples of Jake's earthen dried blood and hair from Shoal Creek overpass, along with Abby's spirit tears were components of the mixture, but certain elements were still lacking.

Jake invited Miranda and a few ancient celebrities who'd attended the Mender harbor bonfire festivities, to come rally around Naomi's cause.

The new venue for the meeting was Naomi's mountain chalet, which was tucked away high atop the Mender mountain range in a secluded primeval meadow. Her guests had to scale the heights of the rugged terrain to reach her hideaway.

Isabella Maestas the Countess of Catalonia, Prince Rinaldo, along with Harrold and Alice, and numerous Gatherer and Mender creatures made the pilgrimage to pay respects and show support.

At dusk, they gathered around an immense fire pit. The frosty air and spicy odor of the mountain cedars stung their nostrils.

Naomi entered the great hearth riding a beautiful white Arabian stallion. The imperially clad beast held its composure as popping embers sailed around the arena.

Naomi dismounted in glorious fashion and climbed the podium. She sucked in a deep breath and spilled forth portentous words.

"I bear witness to truth, oh colleagues. On this fabled starlit night, I urge you to support me in my quest to overthrow the Ruffian fortress which Stella the Diviner commands. I'm done being driven into seclusion at this Mender mountaintop hideaway, so I've given Stella an ultimatum: I'm gonna kick her stealthy ass if she doesn't back the fuck off, pack her bags and depart this sphere forever. Stealing our property and kidnapping Gretchen is disgraceful. Payback's a bitch, though. Our own Murtha the Mender flew a sortie, and has obtained a lock of Stella's hair; I'll personally extract a strand of her DNA in my lab and mutate it into an anti-venom to neutralize her nefarious Ruffian legions. We'll inject the toxin into their habitat before they have time to react, and watch them wither away."

From the smoky shadows a figure appeared. It was Rinaldo, the Spanish knight. "M'Lady, with all due respect, leading an attack into Stella's underworld will likely doom Gretchen, as the odious Stella the Diviner shall perceive it as a personal vendetta and lash back by exterminating innocent lives. At last count, she's abducted hundreds from your regiment; each displays a progressively debilitating form of grief sickness, void of their mates and in severe distress."

Jake, the Countess Isabella and Miranda nodded in agreement to his words.

Naomi recalculated. "Damn then, let me brainstorm...perhaps we give Stella a taste of her own medicine, so to speak."

Her words brought the gathering to the edge of their seats.

Naomi signaled for her bodyguards to bring forth the old chest which contained her ghosts of antiquity.

"I'm willing to unchain these spirits because they operate on a higher dimension than any of my Gatherer or Mender beings."

Miranda was perplexed. "Um, Naomi, isn't Energy Shifting a more potent counterattack to use than these bombastic spirits? I mean, the way Gretchen and I were able to gain access to Lover's Purgatory was through geokinetic invisibility, where we subtly tapped into the Moldavite crystal's power to mask our presence."

"Absolutely not!" Naomi exclaimed. "That merely mimicked invisibility, but its spell wore off once the moon rays diminished, remember? Unboxing these friendly spirits will yield awesome results, because they're capable of *Transcendental Shifting*, the highest form of cloaking and concealment."

Naomi clapped her hands and snapped her fingers three times. Within a brief moment, Murtha and another Mender assisted in lugging over the old wooden trunk.

Naomi fell into a half-conscious state. Her eyes rolled back in her head.

"Spirits of Old, feast your ears and eyes on my request for vengeance, for our Mender nation is vulnerable to Stella the Diviner's leagues of Ruffians who seek to overthrow us. Our best hope is through your intervention."

The crowd cheered in anticipation of what was unfolding.

She raised an ivory sword and spoke concerning the sealed box.

"I hereby release these supernatural effigies! Come prepare yourselves to attack Lover's Purgatory! For your warfare skills are far superior to my legions."

She turned to Jake and placed her open palm on his forehead.

"Jake Conroe, I commission you to take the Mender flask from Miranda and unite with this ghastly band in a quest to free your beloved Gretchen from the yoke of oppression!"

The chest was thrust opened by a whirlwind, spawning a cloud of dust which temporarily blinded the gathering.

Kubernatos the seafaring captain, Ox the Deceiver, Azel the charmer, Tranquillitas the puritan princess, and Adonis and Minerva the flamboyant lovers, were exorcised from the splintery old crate.

"Proceed toward the center of the fire pit, oh specters, and access my portal to your new destination! I grant you all Godspeed!" Naomi said.

25

aomi's phantoms and Jake boarded a Mender bobsled and shot through the portal toward earth. The sensation was like skimming down a greased playground slide with enormous cotton balls coating their bodies.

Bursting through the atmosphere like a reckless meteor, they touched down within the confines of the cemetery. The wild grasses smoldered from the radiation as the group exited and fanned out into strategic positions.

Ox the Deceiver, and Kubernatos the captain, set up an outpost near the Bois d'Arc tree. They transformed into shadow entities to protect the Mender gateway from unwarranted access.

At the gravestones, the spirit-nymph Azel used her talents of seduction to confuse the erotic dancers and Ruffians patrolling the crypts. Azel's supple and arousing kisses easily satisfied their twisted appetites.

Tranquillitas, the gorgeous and peaceable specter, spun a lulling hex over the Ruffian stronghold. Its effects yielded a pacifying plume of false security, turning the above-ground enemy into carefree, blithe spirits. They chilled out so much, many dropped their weapons, initiated poker games, whistled songs and danced jigs.

The grand lovers Adonis and Minerva strutted past them dragging Jake in shackles, posing as Ruffian comrades. They entered Lover's Purgatory after concealing the Virgin Hazing flask under Jake's tunic, along with a magical dagger hidden in his loin holster.

At the interrogation station, believing Jake to be a recaptured prisoner, a Ruffian watchman detained and heckled him. "Look who the cat drug in! Who be *you*, scoundrel?"

Adonis acted his part convincingly. "This is Polyphemus, remember? He's a puny excuse for a man. We caught him fleeing the area! He's *a deserter*, it's written on his face."

While being strip searched, Jake noticed Gretchen's body slumped over in a musty cell close by. She was shivering and disheveled. His acute hearing picked up her faint cries.

"Jake, Jake, oh my Jake..."

The Ruffian inquisitor yanked him by the hair and slammed his face against the slimy cavern walls. "Hey, bloke, I saw you stare at that pretty little wench! How'd you know her?"

Minerva subtly redirected the conversation. "Let's hog tie them together, that pathetic pair deserve each other."

The idea satisfied the steely Ruffian. "Two peas in a pod they are," he contended. "Their secrets will bubble to the surface once we torture them and they beg for mercy."

Adonis and Minerva intensified their playacting to derail the Ruffian's sadistic plans. They jostled Jake around and rammed his body down on the frozen dungeon floor, deliberately close to Gretchen's withered body. The Ruffian snapped a spiked leash collar around his neck and tethered him to the iron bars of the cage.

Jake moaned in fake agony and fell unconsciousness.

All of the ghosts returned above ground to intercept Stella's main army, which had been alerted to the Mender breach, and were swarming the cemetery, marching toward the Mender portal. Her Ruffian infantry were hurling fire bombs at the Bois d'Arc tree in an attempt to destroy the ghosts' escape route back to Naomi.

The Ruffian guards and ghouls inside the dungeon were on high alert, and took up position elsewhere in Lover's Purgatory, leaving Jake, Gretchen and the other prisoners unattended.

When it was safe, Jake wrestled with his handcuffs and gained enough slack to seize his dagger. He struck the powerful Mender blade against his bonds and chains to free himself.

Jake reached out tenderly and stroked Gretchen's hair. His consolation and love for her welled up as a tidal wave, crashing with conviction onto the shore of her heart.

"Babe, it's me, Jake. I hope you can hear my tender plea of longing. I've come here to take you home. Abby and Zach are doing well, thanks to you. Everybody in Saint Germaine is looking for you. Even your doggie Romeo is sulking over your disappearance."

Gretchen's breath was shallow and her skin clammy, but she managed to acknowledge his words by nodding her head a few inches up and down.

"My sweetheart, don't worry," he pleaded. "I'm here to save your plight and replenish your spirit."

Jake took his dagger and sliced a strand of her golden hair, then pulled the Mender flask tucked in his garment and melded the elements together.

"I hereby beckon this Virgin Hazing serum to quench my beloved Gretchen Lanner's thirst. May it manifest within her heart as she consumes its potent properties."

Jake gingerly adjusted her limp head and cajoled her petite, sweet mouth to partake of a mere droplet, but she resisted.

"Oh my dear Jake, please leave me be," she said in a raspy tone. "I'm ready to die and leave this suffering world all behind. We've had a wonderful time celebrating our Indian summer together, but I'll never completely be yours. I've fulfilled my purpose and can't deal with the remorse anymore. I hope you understand."

"Understand what, Gretch? I just extracted a tidbit of your beautiful hair and combined it with my blood from Shoal Creek, completing this powerful celestial love syrup. It's the milk of the Gods to nourish both our souls and transform you into a Virgin Mender princess, ripe as a juicy low-hanging fruit for plucking. All you have to do is drink it."

"I'm afraid it's all a sham, Jake. I'm too guilt ridden to continue living."

"What? C'mon baby, just take a sip and you'll be healed. I assure you that our story isn't going to end like the final scene from Romeo and Juliet."

His comment made Gretchen squeeze out a smirk, but the somber mood returned.

"Look, Jake, I'm drenched in my guilt because I attacked you with the hunting knife and caused your death. You roam around in that Man-God body because you're more divine than human now. I guess it's my only consolation...uh, to know you're safe and..."

"No, Gretch, you have it all wrong! That Tommie entity who texted me at the campsite was Stella in disguise. She baited us; when I was alone and isolated in that truck, driving away like a bat out of hell, she struck. I felt an energy slam down on the gas pedal and make the truck lurch into the other lane. In a split second, head on with that big rig, I knew it was over between us...until Naomi came to visit me in my grave and transformed me. Even Zach was a victim of Stella's perverse games. You lashed out as would anybody, because you lacked the facts. It's not your fault, but I'm here now, sweetheart."

Gretchen was goo-goo eyed and began weeping.

The two embraced and softly kissed.

"Why didn't you tell me all of this earlier, babe?" Gretchen asked.

"Because I didn't know until Miranda returned from Shoal Creek overpass after meeting up with Naomi. It was during the last meeting at the Mender mountaintop where Miranda caught up with me to tell me the sobering news."

An unidentifiable voice yelled out from a cell in the proximity. "Guards, come quick! These two are committing treason! I've witnessed their words, they're both plotting against Stella's realm and are dangerously close to escaping!"

The person was a Ruffian spy planted to flush them out.

The chaotic sounds of swarming, yelling troops in the caves behind them grew stronger and stronger, putting them in imminent danger.

"Hurry, babe, drink the entire contents of this vial and be reconciled to me," Jake begged. "We don't have much time."

"I lack the strength to move my head, darling," she said forlornly.

"No worries..."

His strong hands became her neck brace. He carefully tilted her head into position to receive the Virgin Hazing drink.

"Be my virgin princess, pure and undefiled," he chanted. "From this Mender potion you shall transform into spirit ripeness and become one with your true love, forever indulging in the pleasures of my company."

Gretchen took a slight swallow, then more and more, until she emptied the flask.

As the Ruffians were closing in with their weapons drawn, Jake picked Gretchen up in his arms. A sparkling mist wrapped in the shape of a funnel cloud quickly enveloped them to cloak their escape from the dreaded pit of Lover's Purgatory.

26

The Burkburnett turf wars had begun. The cemetery was lit up like a fireworks show, as the conflict rose to a crescendo between good and evil.

Stella was incensed to learn of Jake and Gretchen's escape from the Ruffian underworld, so she amassed her special forces to put a final whoop ass on Naomi.

The Mender nation had been made vulnerable by the Ruffian ransacking of their storehouses, and were in low supply of combat gear. Naomi's entourage of ghosts counterattacked, reclaiming much of the cemetery. They were an awesome spectacle to behold, wielding spell after spell against the enemy.

Back in Saint Germaine, Gretchen's family, including Callie, Zach, Abby and all her family and friends, were tracking the breaking news of strange weather anomalies being reported at the graveyard. The only manifestations perceptible to the human eye were the gale force winds, rising pockets of hot steam, and random pelting ice storms at play. From the supernatural fifth and sixth dimensions is where the real struggle raged.

A national audience of notable psychics and mediums streamed in to witness the rare spectral events. Everybody was searching for Jake and Gretchen in and around the countryside, interpreting signs and chasing any clues as to their whereabouts.

Jake was nursing Gretchen back to health on his yacht, which was anchored in a secluded cove at the Mender harbor.

"Jake, when will I sprout my hot new body and superhuman powers you said I would acquire after swallowing that magical drink?" Gretchen asked excitedly.

"Patience, my love. You're being transformed into my virgin Mender princess one hair strand at a time."

The couple inched up close to one another, celebrating the sunset as it cast its final rays of crimson over the harbor.

A lonesome white mourning dove appeared on the horizon. Its wings danced on the ocean breezes as it targeted Jake's vessel.

"Life has become good for us, my sweet Gretch. So much to experience, now that you're maturing into the woman I've waited for all these years. Age no longer matters, it's the connection of our spirits which unites us."

On Jake's shoulder the bird landed, unfurling its innocent, irresistible soft coos into his ears. He noticed the bird was clutching a platinum ring with a Moldavite stone setting in its talon. Rolled up and inserted in the stunning jewelry was a miniature scroll.

The little creature brought hope to their embrace. "Must be akin to a homing pigeon," Gretchen mused. "Babe, I think it's come here to deliver a special message to us."

Jake gingerly unrolled the miniature scroll and read aloud.

⌒ ⌒

Hey guys, this is Miranda. Pardon the brief incursion into your privacy, but Naomi asked me to send you her blessings, along with this ring for Gretchen to wear. You should've witnessed the spectacle down here! I

mean, Naomi didn't hold any captives. Those Ruffians were turned into pillars of obsidian, but Stella got away. Cheers to your newfound relationship! Hurry back soon, we'll be waiting for your return!
Love, Miranda.

They felt euphoric and high-fived each other. When the emotions settled, Gretchen looked at Jake with tender eyes. "Hey, babe, one question. Why'd the Virgin Hazing recipe call for my genetic material? And what was all that other stuff mixed in, especially your blood samples? Sounds kinda macabre to me."

"It's a simple recipe, baby," Jake said reflectively. "The collection of tears, blood and hair represent our mutual sacrifice and power to overcome all odds to be one, in spite of your own refusal to believe in yourself. I'm here now, and will never forsake you."

As the enigmatic dove flew away into the clouds, the two lovebirds smooched and reminisced about their earlier life in Saint Germaine, how fate interceded to bring them together in spite of the pain of enduring temporal existence. "There's a silver lining in every storm cloud if you look close enough," Jake asserted. "Whenever you feel a pocket of cold air on a sultry, summer night, somebody may be trying to get your attention."

Suddenly, a twitching, erogenous sensation spread across Gretchen's body. Her breasts went supple and her nipples erect, suck-able and playful. Now tight abs, ripples of muscles replaced the flab. A warm throbbing desire, searching for satisfaction. Purified, glowing skin.

"Damn! Déjà vu all over again! I'm gonna soak up these memories, no more traveling alone anymore!" she proclaimed.

Twilight fell upon the bay as their vibes of love escalated. The hypnotic sound of the lapping waves against the yacht synchronized with the ebb and flow of their own heartbeats.

Platinum dolphins turned backflips and chattered in a language reserved only for royalty. Gretchen and Jake were such royalty, prince and princess of the Mender habitat, taking their rightful places on the throne of soul mate love. The kingdom was theirs to relish and conquer without interruption.

Vibrant, untamed and limitless love.

Jake brought forth two gold goblets and topped them off with vintage French Bordeaux wine. He raised the anchor and toasted to their soul mate love. "Here's to us, side by side in this new brave world, exploring our destiny and never looking in the rear view mirror again to second guess things! Besides, baby, you'll have your wings soon. I'll help you use them when the time is right..."

About the Author

J K Aston is an emerging author of paranormal romance, whose story-telling provides rare insight into the fragile yet profound relationship between humanity's struggles and the hopeful world to come.

www.ingramcontent.com/pod-product-compliance
Lightning Source LLC
Chambersburg PA
CBHW030633130626
46552CB00002B/832